NEXT EXIT

J. A. Springs

I0636838

NEXT EXIT

J. A. Springs

WRITING
FOR THE
WORLD

PRESS

since
2021

Copyright © 2025 Writing for the World Press, LLC.
Lancaster, PA. 17603
All rights reserved.
ISBNs-13:
978-1-966464-02-0 (eBook)
978-1-966464-09-9 (Paperback)

No part of this publication may be reproduced, distributed, or transmitted in any form or by any means, including photocopying, recording, or other electronic or mechanical methods, without the prior written permission of the publisher, except as permitted under U.S. copyright law. For permission requests, contact Writing for the World Press at writingfortheworldpress.com.

This is a work of fiction. Names, characters, places, and incidents are the product of the author's imagination or are used fictitiously. Any resemblance to actual persons, living or dead, or actual events is purely coincidental.

Always for J.M.S. First

Part One

Chapter One

The summer sun hung lazily in the sky, drifting toward the horizon with unhurried ease. Its fading warmth stretched across the quarry, casting everything in a soft golden haze. The jagged rocks, fierce and imposing at midday, now seemed gentler, their edges rounding beneath the evening light. Below, the still water reflected the sky like polished glass, disturbed only by the occasional ripple of a passing breeze.

Laughter bounced between the quarry walls as six children played near the shore, their joy bright and uncomplicated. They splashed each other, chased one another through the shallows, and clung to the last carefree days before high school would scatter their routines and pull them toward Ionia's crowded hallways.

Among them were Stephanie and Chris. Stephanie, fair-skinned with a single dimple tucked into her right cheek, adjusted her glasses as she flicked a handful of water at him. Her green eyes sparkled with mischief. Her blue one-piece swimsuit hugged her frame, and her long hair sat knotted in a bun at the back of her head.

Chris—tall, warm-skinned, and effortlessly charismatic—grinned back at her. Water gleamed across his ebony skin and vibrant green trunks, outlining the subtle flex of his muscles. Every movement between them became a kind of dance, sending brief rainbows arcing through the air when the light hit just right. Whenever she drifted close, Stephanie fit perfectly in the circle of his arms, a fact Chris didn't bother hiding that he enjoyed.

Not far away, Henry perched on a flat rock, applying suntan lotion to his pale skin with exacting care. His dusty blonde hair fell into his eyes, refusing to be tamed. Beside him sat John—lean, muscled, and always ready with a joke. The faint scar across his chin caught the sunlight as he laughed, the last remnant of a childhood mishap involving a rope, a treehouse, and an afternoon neither boy ever forgot.

A little farther up the bank sat Quinn and Babs. Barbie in name and almost in appearance, Babs radiated a bubbly charm that seemed permanently dialed up. She giggled each time Henry so much as glanced her way, and Henry—oblivious or pretending to be—kept his eyes anywhere but on her. Quinn, with her short dark hair and reserved manner, hovered at the edges of things, but her quietness never pushed her out of the group. They always made sure she was included, and Quinn valued that more than she ever said aloud.

This was their circle—closer than most families, bound by years of shared summers, shared jokes, shared secrets. They'd all convinced themselves they were different from other friend groups.

Stronger.

Unbreakable.

They believed they could survive anything if they stayed together.

As the sun dipped lower, their shadows stretched long across the rocks. Henry and John began gathering towels and backpacks. Babs slipped on her sandals. Quinn brushed sand off her legs. One by one, they turned toward Chris and Stephanie, waiting for the pair to rejoin them.

Chris finally caught the hint and clasped Stephanie's hand. They made their way back toward the group to say their goodbyes before heading to the bonfire later that evening. Chris mentioned wanting one last jump from the quarry rim before leaving. John and Henry nodded, already accustomed to Chris's ritual leap. Babs threw Stephanie a playful wink, tugged Quinn along, and the group headed toward home.

Stephanie followed Chris up the steep, craggy slope toward the "jumping rock," a natural ledge hanging twenty-five feet above the quarry's deep pool. Every friend had jumped from it—everyone except

Stephanie. Even Henry, slight and sun-shy, had done it once, urged forward by John's relentless encouragement.

The rule for the jump was simple: a kiss before the leap. One thrill before the next.

Chris stopped at the edge and faced her, taking her hands. The evening breeze had dried the water from his skin, and the warmth of the sun lingered in him. He smiled at her—wide, genuine, and so handsome it made her chest tighten. Stephanie never quite understood why a boy like Chris had chosen her. Girls at school practically lined up for him, while she considered herself plain, glasses and all.

"Are you ready?" he asked, his voice low and steady. "You've got to do it at least once before summer ends."

"Why?" she whispered, unable to hold his gaze for long.

Chris stepped closer, softening. "Because you're brave, girl. Stronger than you know." He kissed her forehead gently.

"I don't feel strong," she murmured, turning away.

He lifted her chin with a careful touch. "I know you are," he said, then kissed her lightly on the lips. Stephanie's eyes fluttered closed, her lips lingering.

"If you want more," he teased, "you'll have to follow me."

"That's not fair," she complained, pouting.

"It's just you and me," he said with a quiet laugh.

"Yeah," she breathed.

"Then come and get me." He kissed her cheek—and jumped.

She gasped, startled by his sudden leap. And then—before she could overthink it—she followed, her hand still gripping his.

They hit the water with a splash, Stephanie's scream ending in a mouthful of quarry water. She surfaced sputtering, scanning for Chris. When she spotted him, she smacked the water in mock outrage, sending a splash directly into his smug grin.

"You're a jerk," she grumbled.

Chris swam toward her, and when she wrapped her arms around his neck, he led them both back to shore. They sprawled on the rocks, their bodies warm against the cooling air.

The horizon glowed red and orange, the last of the sunlight stretching long and thin through the atmosphere. Stephanie tugged Chris closer until he rolled atop her, bracing himself with his hands. She cupped his face between her palms.

"You have a beautiful heart, Stephanie," he said, smiling down at her.

She returned the smile. "Only because people like you let me show it."

"I'll be your lucky penny if you'll be my four-leaf clover," he said softly.

"Okay."

She kissed him deeply, their lips and tongues moving together in the fading light. When they parted, Chris brushed her cheek with his thumb.

"If you were an angel," he said, "I'd bind your wings so you'd never fly away."

Stephanie's eyes softened. "You wouldn't have to. If I were an angel, I'd give them up just to stay with you."

He kissed her again, then lay beside her. She rested her head on his arm, curling close.

"What's on your mind?" she asked quietly.

"You," he said. "Us. All of us." He reached toward the sky as if plucking at the first emerging stars. "I want to give you everything. The moon, the stars. The whole world."

She shook her head gently. "Just give me you."

He didn't answer at first. Then her hand guided his face back toward hers, and he smiled.

"I can do that," he said. He stood, offering her his hand. "Come on. Let's get to the bonfire."

The "bonfire" took place in Henry's backyard, where a modest fire pit glowed beneath the darkening sky. The six friends had planned nothing extravagant—just sodas, popcorn, s'mores, and the easy laughter that belonged to teenagers who still believed time was theirs to spend freely.

By the time Chris and Stephanie rounded the side of the house, the others were already gathered in a loose circle around the flames. No one had been waiting on them, but their arrival was met with warm calls and cheerful smiles.

"Hey, you two!" Babs sang, waving them over. Chris and Stephanie slipped into the open chairs without hesitation, the fire's warmth embracing them along with the familiarity of their friends.

Stephanie found herself seated between Babs and Chris; on Babs's far side sat Henry, then John, and finally Quinn. It was their usual, comfortable order—one they fell into without planning.

"So," Babs asked Stephanie in a conspiratorial whisper, "what did you two get up to after we left?"

Stephanie flushed immediately. Before she could stumble through an answer, Chris stepped in.

"I made Stephanie take the jump off the rock."

A small eruption of applause and approving noises followed. Stephanie ducked her head, wishing briefly she could disappear behind her own glasses. Everyone knew the rule about jumping from the rock—and the kiss that came first. Everyone had done it at least once. Stephanie had been the last holdout.

"Great job, Stephanie," John said, giving her an encouraging grin. He nudged Henry. "She did great, didn't she?"

Henry nodded, smiling warmly. "Yeah. Congrats, brave girl."

As Stephanie looked around the fire at each familiar face, she saw nothing but pride and affection reflecting back—fire-lit smiles glowing almost brighter than the flames themselves. Almost. Quinn alone avoided her gaze, staring fixedly into the fire as if it held answers Stephanie wasn't meant to see.

Stephanie felt a small pinch in her chest. It would have meant so much if Quinn had simply looked at her—just acknowledged her. But before that ache could settle, Chris's voice cut through the quiet chatter, pulling everyone's attention as easily as ever.

"Wow," Chris said, leaning back in his chair. "How long have we all been friends?"

He wasn't asking anyone in particular, but Henry answered anyway.

"For some of us, since fourth or fifth grade."

He was mostly right. Quinn had been the last to join, arriving at the start of middle school—new to the city, new to everything. They'd all been drawn to her gentleness, adopting her before she even realized she'd been folded into their group. It helped her find her footing, and they never once made her feel like an outsider.

Chris waved a hand dismissively. "Two years, ten years—doesn't matter. All I know is I'm gonna be friends with you guys forever."

The fire crackled softly. Every one of them nodded in agreement, the unspoken truth settling warm and solid between them. When Chris's gaze finally landed on Stephanie, he paused. She seemed to glow—whether from the fire, from his affection, or some combination, he couldn't decide.

Suddenly, Chris clapped his hands. "I think we should make a pact. Next year we're all starting high school together, so let's promise we'll stay friends for all four years. No matter what."

"I like that idea," John said immediately. Then, as always, he checked with Henry. "You like it, right?"

Henry nodded so hard his glasses shifted down his nose. "Yeah. Sounds good."

Babs clapped, her braces catching the firelight like tiny sparks. "I think it's perfect, Chris." She turned. "What about you, Quinn?"

Quinn startled at being addressed. For a moment she seemed unsure whether the question was meant for her at all. But with everyone's eyes suddenly on her, she whispered, "It sounds good to me."

Her soft voice prompted a ripple of laughter—not unkind, just affectionate—and the conversation moved forward again, circling around the idea of a pact and all that the next four years might bring. Four years of growing, changing, discovering who they would become under pressure from the outside world.

But tonight, the future felt bright and reachable. Their paths lay open like roads drawn in starlight.

"Is everyone agreed?" Chris asked finally.

One by one, each friend nodded.

And just like that, their pact was sealed in the glow of the fire—six hands warming in the same circle of light, six hearts convinced nothing could break what they had.

Chapter Two

Stephanie moved through the long hallway, lockers rising on either side like mute sentries. Her mission was simple—reach her first afternoon class—but the post-lunch haze made each step feel like wading through warm air. Trigonometry waited for her ahead: demanding, unforgiving, and essential for the mathematics degree she dreamed of. She couldn't afford to drift.

She was a few doors away when two hands suddenly covered her eyes. She didn't need to guess. Only one person in the entire school touched her that way.

"Hey, Babs," Stephanie laughed, her voice carrying over the crowded corridor.

"You always guess right," Babs whined dramatically, stomping one foot as if wounded. Her high-pitched voice turned even her mock-anger into something bright.

Stephanie slowed until Babs fell into step beside her. "It's always you. No one else would dare."

As they walked, Stephanie noticed—like she always did—how the flow of students seemed to bend around Babs. People noticed her. They always had. Stephanie, by contrast, moved through the currents unseen, a quiet presence slipping past louder currents.

High school had transformed Babs from the shy girl with braces and thick glasses into someone everyone knew. Her older sister—the head cheerleader—helped open doors, but Babs had been the one to carry herself through them. Braces were long gone, glasses replaced by laser surgery, and her smile—always warm—had grown unmistakably radiant.

But what mattered most to Stephanie was what hadn't changed. Beneath all the attention, Babs was still Babs. Loyal. Steady. Hers. The idea of losing her—even to something as natural as growing up—was a fear Stephanie kept locked away.

They had barely gone another ten paces when Stephanie's breath caught.

Chris was walking toward them.

Her heart thudded painfully, every practiced layer of calm peeling back.

'There he is,' she thought, a familiar ache blooming low in her chest. The one who used to be my closest friend.

Distance had grown between them—quietly, steadily—and she never understood when that shift had begun. Or why.

Babs noticed instantly. Without hesitation, she slipped a hand around Stephanie's arm and wove their fingers together, pulling Stephanie close until their shoulders brushed. The gesture was subtle but solid, a silent vow of support.

Across the hallway, Chris's attention flickered toward them. In the same instant, he lifted his arm and draped it around the shoulders of the girl walking beside him.

Quinn.

Caught off guard, Quinn glanced up at him. Chris never did public affection. Not in years. Not with her.

She followed his gaze—straight down the hallway, straight toward Stephanie.

Her stomach tightened.

Chris wasn't pulling her close because he wanted to. He was pulling her close because Stephanie was watching.

Heat crept up Quinn's neck. She dropped her eyes to the tiles, suddenly fascinated by their scuffed patterns, trying to hide the way realization stung.

Chris was performing.

And she was the prop.

Chris slowed as he reached them, bringing Quinn to a halt beside him. The moment felt staged—almost choreographed—and Quinn's instinct was to shrink, to fade out of sight before anyone noticed how uncomfortable she was.

"Hey," Chris said to Stephanie.

The smile he wore wasn't the one she remembered from childhood. The easy warmth had drained out long ago, replaced with something sharper—resentment, maybe. Hurt. A boy who'd once been promised the world and now lived in the rubble of whatever broke.

"Hi, Chris," Stephanie replied, her voice threaded with a sadness she tried to hide. Every part of her felt the empty space where their friendship used to live.

She turned to Quinn. "Hi, Quinn."

There was hope in that small greeting—hope for some flicker of the closeness they once shared.

"Hey," Quinn mumbled.

She lifted a hand to remove Chris's arm, but his grip tightened—subtle at first, then firm enough for her shoulder to ache. Quinn stilled, breath caught between annoyance and something colder. His hold wasn't affectionate. It was deliberate. A message for Stephanie.

And Quinn was the delivery mechanism.

She looked around the hallway as if searching for an exit. There wasn't one—not from his arm, not from the eyes she felt grazing over her, not from the uneasy knot twisting in her stomach.

Beside Stephanie, Babs stiffened.

Her discomfort wasn't only about what she was seeing now. The fissures between all four of them had roots—old ones. Staying loyal to Stephanie had felt, at times, like choosing a side she never wanted to choose. Chris and Quinn had pulled away years ago, and Babs carried a quiet guilt over the separation she hadn't caused but couldn't fix.

The split had begun when Chris disappeared during their freshman year. They'd all known something was wrong, but none of them said it aloud.

He'd been held back a grade—officially for attendance. Unofficially, because he'd been fighting a war at home no one could see.

His father's drinking had long been a threat, but when Chris's mother left, his father's cruelty sharpened. He masked it behind the lie of 'boxing training,' a story no one questioned too closely. The bruises, the swollen ribs, the blackened eyes—they were supposed to be from sparring.

They weren't.

Chris had come back to school carrying those scars, trying to pretend they meant nothing. But his absence from the group was the beginning of the end. Without him, their tight circle loosened. Without his steady presence, the laughter echoed differently. Eventually the threads snapped.

And when they did, Quinn was the one who didn't drift. She broke into a sprint.

In Stephanie's mind, Quinn had run straight to Chris—clinging to him with fierce loyalty, orbiting him so tightly that the rest of them couldn't get close even if they tried. He had become her anchor in a world she didn't trust.

The painful truth was simpler:

Once Chris left them, Quinn left too.

And neither of them ever really came back.

Stephanie still felt the sting.

Even after she and Chris had finally admitted their feelings for each other, he had drifted—slipped out of her grasp and into Quinn's orbit. It hurt more than she ever wanted to admit. It felt like rejection wrapped in silence, a dismissal of everything they'd once been brave enough to say aloud.

But what could she do?

Some things you can't pull back once they've slipped away.

All she could do now was feel it, face it, and keep moving.

Chris had pushed away from all of them, not just her. They knew the reasons—his home life, his father, the darkness he lived with—but knowing didn't mean any of them had managed to stop his retreat. Stephanie was one of them. Even loving him hadn't given her the courage to reach out before he walled himself off.

He never gave them an opening anyway.

His silence was the door he kept locked.

Eventually Chris guided Quinn back into the surge of students, his hand still at her shoulder. His parting "See ya" blended into the hallway noise until it vanished entirely.

Stephanie watched until they disappeared into the crowd. Only then did she let out the breath she'd been holding, swallowing the ache that sat heavy under her ribs. She wished—for the thousandth time—that things had gone differently. That the bonds they once shared hadn't splintered. That Chris hadn't needed to retreat at all.

A gentle tug on her arm drew her back.

"Come on, girl," Babs murmured. "We're gonna be late, and you know Mr. Walker hates tardy."

The practicality of the statement snapped Stephanie out of her spiral. She forced a smile and let Babs pull her forward. By the time they reached the classroom wing, the weight on her chest had loosened enough for her to joke.

"Why are you even taking trigonometry, Babs?" she teased, leaning against her locker. "You hate math."

Babs grinned, bright as ever. "Because it was the only class I could get with you this year."

Stephanie snorted. "That is the dumbest reason. You're literally failing."

"I am holding onto a strong D," Babs corrected with mock dignity, tapping her chest as if making a pledge. "And I'd be pulling a solid C if my best friend tutored me more than once every three years."

Stephanie sighed—dramatically, but affectionately. "Fine. I'll come by more often. You're still crazy."

Babs shrugged, fully unbothered. "A D or higher gets me the credit, professor."

Their laughter followed them all the way into class. An hour and fifteen minutes later, they stepped back into the hallway, splitting off almost immediately.

"Text me before our study session," Babs called out, already being absorbed into a cluster of her cheer squad friends.

"I will," Stephanie promised.

Watching Babs join the tide of popular faces, Stephanie felt a faint tug at her heart—the separation of paths, the divergence she couldn't stop even if she wanted to. But there was also comfort. Babs always came back to her.

Stephanie hurried to her locker, letting the rhythm of the hallway guide her. Her body navigated the crowd on instinct while her mind drifted elsewhere.

Back to the hallway.

Back to that moment.

Back to Chris.

She replayed it—his voice, his expression, the tension in Quinn's shoulders, the shadow behind his smile. It looped through her thoughts with unwelcome clarity, each detail vivid, like the memory refused to dim.

Once, his smile had been effortless. Beautiful.

Now, there was something missing in it—something that made her chest pinch every time she saw him.

Regret tugged at Stephanie as she walked—an ache for the paths she and Chris never took, for the friendship that faded, for the love that had slipped away. She wanted it back. All of it. But the way forward felt impossibly far, like trying to stitch together something long torn.

Her thoughts drifted so deeply that her feet stopped paying attention. She collided with someone—books jostling, apologies tangling—and looked up into a familiar, boyish face from her past.

Henry Goldman.

He blinked as if waking from the same daze. "Excuse me—sorry," he muttered, then finally focused. "Oh. Hi, Step."

Only he ever called her that.

"Hey, Henry," she replied softly.

He shifted awkwardly, that old nervous energy still clinging to him. "What're you up to?"

Stephanie lifted her trig textbook. "Study hall. Computer lab."

Henry's shoulders relaxed, and for a second he looked like the boy she remembered—awkward, yes, but comfortably so.

"You're the smartest person I know in math," he said. "So why use a computer for trigonometry?"

"I'm not," she said, amused. "Just using the online part of the textbook."

Henry pushed his glasses up. "You really don't need it. Computers are just giant calculators. I'd rather do everything by hand." Then, with a faint smile: "They're pretty dumb at math anyway."

Stephanie blinked. "How so?"

"They only add two numbers—"

"Zeros and ones," they finished together.

Their laughter came easily—unexpectedly easy—washing away the years of distance like chalk wiped from a board.

"We haven't cracked that joke in forever," Stephanie said, wiping her eyes.

"Yeah," Henry agreed. "Way too long."

Another voice chimed in, warm and familiar.

"Hiya, Mr. Gold."

John.

He strode up wearing his letter jacket and easy confidence, dusty blond hair tousled just right. Over the summer before freshman year, he'd grown taller, stronger—suddenly popular. Suddenly not Henry's shadow anymore.

And Stephanie hated the change more than she admitted.

She looked back at Henry and felt her stomach twist. He'd gone stiff—ramrod straight, like a board had been strapped to his spine. His face was carefully blank, eyes a little too wide.

John slid in beside him, barely acknowledging Stephanie beyond a flick of attention that said clearly: We're not friends anymore.

Or at least, not around the two larger guys standing behind him.

"You're hard to track down, Mr. Gold," John said lightly. "Thought I told you to meet me at my locker. Didn't wanna carry all these books."

The guys behind him laughed. Loudly. Pointlessly.

Stephanie's pulse tightened. She recognized the tone—sharp under the playfulness. She prayed it wouldn't turn into another painful moment like earlier.

Henry swallowed. "I've got my own stuff to carry, John."

The air shifted.

John stepped in close. Forehead nearly touching Henry's. The smile gone.

"You're embarrassing me in front of my friends," he murmured. "And what did I tell you? Call me 'J' at school. Don't talk back. Makes me look weak."

Then—smack.

John hit the books in Henry's arms hard enough to send them spilling across the floor, scattering in every direction.

"There. Now your hands are free." He slung his own book bag onto Henry's shoulder—another quiet humiliation. "Catch you in class, buddy."

As John passed, he slammed his shoulder into Henry. The two others mimicked him, each delivering their own shove. One even kicked the fallen books, sending them skidding farther down the hall.

Henry stood frozen.

Stephanie felt something hot coil through her—anger, disbelief, helplessness. All tangled.

And rising.

Henry kept his eyes down, tears slipping into the corners despite his effort to hide them. Stephanie didn't comment. Instead, she crouched immediately and began gathering his books, giving him the space to pretend nothing had happened. While he readjusted his crooked glasses, she pretended not to notice the quick swipe beneath his eyes.

Together, they organized the scattered books into a neat stack. Stephanie helped settle them into his arms before finally speaking.

"Why do you let him treat you like that?"

Henry didn't answer.

"Henry," she urged gently, trying to meet his eyes.

He refused, turning away as if hoping the conversation would dissolve behind him.

"Henry?" she called again as he walked.

He paused—head low, shoulders tight. "Just leave it alone, Step." His voice was frayed, thin. Then he kept going.

Stephanie watched him disappear into the shifting crowd, feeling the quiet sting of another friendship slipping out of reach. Chris, Quinn, now Henry—all fracturing in the same strange pattern. And all of it seemed to trace back to the moment Chris faded from their group.

She made it through her study session in the computer lab, pushing aside her emotions until the last school bell finally released her. On the walk home, she called Babs, and they agreed to meet for a study night. Stephanie went straight to her house.

Babs greeted her at the door with her usual brightness and ushered her upstairs. They spread their books across the bedroom floor, the familiar rhythm of equations and notes giving Stephanie something to anchor herself to. Only after they finished did she let herself bring up what had been weighing on her.

"Babs... what happened between you and Henry?" Stephanie asked. "Back in freshman year, you two were inseparable. You looked happy. And then it... stopped. You never said why."

Babs's smile faltered, replaced by something soft and wounded. She sat back against the bed, hands resting in her lap.

"He didn't want to date me because he's a good guy," she said quietly. "He thought he was too boring for someone like me. Said someone like John would be a better fit."

Stephanie stared at her, incredulous. "That's ridiculous. Why would he say something like that?"

"Because he didn't feel worthy," Babs whispered. Her eyes shimmered. "I told him a hundred times that I didn't want anyone else. But he couldn't believe it."

Her voice cracked. "I miss him so much, Stephanie. I love him. And watching John treat him like trash—" She shook her head, swallowing back tears. "I just wish things would go back to how they were."

Stephanie wrapped her arms around her in a tight hug. "I do too," she murmured. Her mind drifted, unbidden, to Chris. "I miss all of them."

Babs managed a small, watery laugh. "You say that—but you're still hung up on your guy."

Stephanie nudged her with a halfhearted shove. "You're impossible."

"You know I'm right," Babs said, wiping her cheeks. She leaned her head against the edge of the bed, eyes red but calmer. "You can't pretend you don't miss Chris too."

Stephanie didn't answer.

Babs already knew the truth.

Instead, Stephanie lunged and started tickling her until Babs shrieked, the tension finally breaking like a snapped string.

Chapter Three

Quinn spent twenty minutes weaving through staff entrances and maintenance hallways, slipping past teachers with the ease of someone who'd practiced this routine far too often. She finally found Chris behind the gym, sitting on the low concrete ledge that overlooked the track. It was the same place he always went when he decided class didn't matter and a cigarette did.

He didn't look up. He just closed the worn leather book in his hands, slid it into his pocket, and took another slow drag.

"What do you want?"

Quinn stopped four feet away, eyes on the ground. She didn't speak. She never did—not until he told her to come closer.

Chris let her stand there. He even tried to ignore her long enough to make her leave, but ten minutes passed before he finally caved. "Come here."

She stepped forward immediately.

Up close, she lifted a hand toward the bruise blossoming around his right eye. He caught her wrist before she could touch him. Before he decided he would pull her down so she sat between his legs.

"Leave it alone," he muttered.

Quinn withdrew her hand and as she moved, her foot slipped on the concrete.

Chris reached out to steady her, but his hand shot out too fast, catching her mid-fall — and sliding, by pure mistake, beneath the hem of her skirt.

A sudden tug, a soft tearing sound, and Quinn froze.

Chris recoiled as if burned, staring at his hand, then yanking it back to his chest.

His face tightened in mortification.

"You ripped them," she murmured, feeling the satin slip down her thigh.

Quinn glanced down, then up at him, giving the smallest shake of her head — not angry, not embarrassed, just silently telling him it's fine.

She steadied herself, then lowered into place between his legs as though nothing had happened.

Once settled, she shifted—small movements he couldn't interpret. Eventually she turned partially and pressed something small, warm, and soft into his palm. He glanced down at the balled up material. Silk. Pink. He turned away from her, slipping the torn fabric into his pocket.

"Sorry," he mumbled.

Quinn said nothing. She leaned back instead.

The tension in her body hummed until he set a hand on her neck—a gesture meant to establish control more than comfort. Her whole posture loosens the moment he does. He flicked his cigarette away, exhaled smoke, and watched her absorb the sting of it without complaint.

His phone vibrated in his pocket. He dropped his hand and Quinn folded forward like a puppet whose strings had been cut, waiting.

"Yeah," Chris said into the phone. "I'll get the rest of them. Eight or eight-thirty."

He hung up and set his palm against her throat again, thumb resting under her jaw. Quinn inhaled sharply. That reaction—her complete surrender to the slightest pressure—was something he hated himself for understanding so well.

Her breath caught and sped. He could feel every beat of her pulse beneath his hand.

At first, she reached back to touch him, sliding her hand to his waistband. That was when he caught her ponytail and tugged gently to stop her.

"Not now," he said.

Quinn froze, eyes down, waiting—always waiting—for whatever version of him would speak next.

He finally let her go. She stood shakily, smoothing her skirt. Chris rose behind her, the air between them thick with everything they refused to say.

"You're messed up in the head," he muttered.

"So are you," Quinn said quietly.

His jaw tightened. "Did your parents start up again last night? Telling you that you need to be the perfect girl? The best daughter?"

Quinn glared. He took the look as confirmation.

"I figured," he said.

She shot back, "Maybe your dad only had to tell you once."

His fist twitched, rising before he caught himself. For a moment, neither moved. Quinn didn't flinch—didn't even blink. She was daring him. Begging him.

"You're really twisted," he said, lowering his hand. Not because of her—because of himself.

Quinn's gaze softened. "Who was that on the phone?"

"Why?" he asked. "If it was a girl, would you care?"

"No," she said simply.

"Yes you would."

Quinn shook her head. "I was mad because you used me to hurt Stephanie. That wasn't fair—to her or to me."

Chris grabbed her arm as she tried to step back. The motion wasn't violent, just sharp enough to make her stop. Smoke curled from his lips again as he exhaled near her face.

He stared at her, fury simmering behind his eyes. Not at her—never at her. At everything else. At himself.

Quinn finally looked away.

Chris released her. "Thought so."

He checked the time, shoved his hands into his pockets, and headed toward the parking lot. Quinn followed automatically. When she asked, "Are you going to the pep rally?" he stopped, shot her a look that could curdle paint, and growled, "Just come on."

He walked faster. She kept up easily.

He looked back once. Only once. Her eyes were already on him.

That, somehow, unsettled him more than anything.

She had attached herself to him the moment he crawled out of the pit he'd disappeared into—after the bruises got worse, after the anger started eating him alive, after he'd pushed everyone else away. She never left. Never let go.

And deep down, he knew the truth:

He wasn't in control of whatever existed between them.

She was.

Stephanie caught up with Babs as the pep rally ended. With school finally over, they decided to slip off campus for a quick bite before returning for the homecoming game that evening.

The field soon claimed Babs—her cheer uniform already half-hidden beneath her jacket—while Stephanie settled into the stands. Her cheers were more for her friend than for the team.

During the game, her gaze drifted to the sidelines where Henry and John stood together. Seeing Henry in football gear still felt strange; he didn't fit the mold for contact sports. But as a kicker he was unmatched, outscoring John by a mile. From her distance it looked like the two boys were arguing, though she couldn't make out a word.

She didn't try to. Their friendship had dissolved long ago, and whatever storm brewed between them was no longer her concern. She turned her attention back to the field.

The game was predictable from the outset—Ionia High trounced their opponents 55–0. John scored twice; Henry nailed every point-after and a few field goals. When the final whistle blew, Babs found her again, and the two began the fifteen-minute walk home.

Passing cars honked in celebration, kids leaning out windows and waving.

Most students headed to the little restaurant downtown—the one that might as well have been frozen in the 1950s, thanks to its hand-spun milkshakes and decent burgers. But Stephanie and Babs preferred the walk. It wasn't the lack of a ride, nor the mild chill in the air. It was simply the chance to unwind together.

"I noticed John and Henry on the sidelines," Stephanie said.

"Really? Were you looking for them?" Babs asked, attempting nonchalance while practically vibrating with interest.

"I wasn't looking for anyone. I just happened to see them."

Babs clasped her hands behind her back, smiling into the sidewalk. "So... was there anything in particular you were hoping to 'happen to' see when you 'happened to' spot them?"

Stephanie laughed softly. "If you're asking whether I was looking for Chris—no. I just saw Henry and John arguing."

Babs's gaze dropped. Her voice thinned to a whisper. "They were arguing about me."

"What? Why? How do you know?"

"John came up to me before the game and asked me to the homecoming dance. I told him I was going with Henry. He stormed off."

Stephanie blinked, startled. "Are you going with Henry?"

Babs didn't answer.

"Babs?"

She exhaled. "I meant to ask him. I think John likes me... but he's always felt like Henry's little brother to me. I can't see him any other way. And I think Henry knows that. I think he's pulling back so I'll give John a chance."

"If you still love Henry, why don't you just talk to him?" Stephanie pressed. "You know he cared about you."

Babs's tone wavered. "You say that so easily. But what about you?"

Stephanie frowned. "What about me?"

"What about you and Chris, Steph? Before freshman year, you two finally stopped dancing around each other. You were... beautiful together. We all wanted a love like yours." Babs twisted her fingers together, her voice soft with memory. "And then six months later he disappeared and everything fell apart. So why aren't you trying to fix things? You still love him."

Stephanie looked away, the street lamps catching in her hair. "Chris pulled away and practically shoved me out of his life. I tried. He made it impossible."

"That's how I feel about Henry."

Stephanie snorted. "Yeah, but Henry didn't vanish for half a year."

Babs opened her mouth to respond, but a car slowed beside them. She leaned toward Stephanie. "Speak of the devil."

The passenger window rolled down, revealing Quinn. True to form, she didn't look at either girl; she murmured a quiet "Hi," shy as ever.

"Hi, Quinn," the two girls echoed.

A deep voice drifted from the driver's seat. Stephanie and Babs leaned down to see Chris looking back at them.

"Where are you guys headed?" Chris asked.

Stephanie froze, uncertain if she was more surprised to see him again or to hear him speak to her at all. Her eyes flicked to Quinn before she could answer. Quinn's gaze was wide and soft—then Stephanie saw it.

The torn pink panties.

Folded on the bench seat between Quinn and Chris.

Quinn's face blanched. She balled the ripped fabric into her fist and slid it under her thigh. When she looked back at Stephanie, the pain in her eyes was unmistakable. She dropped her gaze immediately.

Babs, unaware, answered Chris's question. "We're just walking home. Did you guys go to the game?"

Chris lounged back, one arm draped behind the seat. He noticed Quinn's panic. He noticed Stephanie noticing it. He pretended he didn't. His voice was calm, almost smug.

"We didn't go to the game. We were busy doing... other things."

Quinn stared at her lap.

Chris reached past her, unlocked the passenger door, and pushed it open. "Get in the back."

Quinn froze. A flicker of panic crossed her face, but Chris's expression was unreadable. She obeyed, climbing out, pulling the seat forward, and slipping silently into the back.

"Get in," he told Babs and Stephanie.

The girls exchanged a look. Stephanie's stomach twisted. This felt wrong.

"John called before the game," Chris added, voice smooth. "He wants the whole gang together again."

Still they hesitated.

Babs's thoughts jumped ahead. "Is Henry going to be there?"

Chris flashed his old, charismatic smile. "Yeah. He rode with John."

Babs lit up. She turned to Stephanie, who looked sick with doubt. "C'mon. It'll be fine. Maybe things can go back to how they were."

Babs climbed into the back beside Quinn. Stephanie stood motionless until Chris patted the passenger seat.

Against her instincts, she got in, buckled her seatbelt, and Chris pulled away from the curb.

Part Two

Chapter Four

Chris guided the car onto the nearest entrance ramp leading to the state road, the engine humming as he accelerated north.

Stephanie, noticing they were putting real distance between their homes, nudged Babs to call her parents. It felt responsible—one less thing to worry about when they didn't return at the usual time.

Call done, phone away, Stephanie finally had a moment to take in the car around her.

This was her first time in Chris's prized project. The vintage two-door Chevy had been restored almost entirely by his own hands. It was immaculate—modern radio, digital dash, soft interior lighting—woven seamlessly into the classic bones of the vehicle.

She wanted to compliment him.

But as she turned toward him to speak, the bright streak of pink caught her eye again.

Quinn's torn panties were still on the seat.

Quinn had hidden them earlier under her leg but hadn't slipped them into her pocket. They lay there, impossible to ignore. Stephanie's stomach tightened. Questions she didn't want answers to stirred up anyway.

Chris followed her line of sight. His expression flicked, then smoothed.

Without a word, he reached over, scooped up the fabric, and extended his hand behind him.

Quinn accepted the ruined panties quickly, cheeks pink, and tucked them into her jacket pocket just before Babs shifted her attention from the window.

Stephanie turned away, back to the glass. Outside was nothing but navy-blue blur—dark trees rushing past, swallowed by cold fog creeping off the roadside. The sky was starless tonight, the moon hidden behind a heavy ceiling of clouds.

She drifted so far inward that she didn't hear her name at first.

"Welcome back, stranger," Chris said, a small smile tugging at his mouth.

Stephanie startled and returned the smile. "Sorry. I didn't hear you."

"I had to call you a few times. Where'd you go?"

She shrugged. "Nowhere. Just thinking."

"What about?"

Her stomach tightened again. She waited out the knot of nerves before speaking.

"Are you... happy with Quinn?"

Chris flicked his eyes to the rearview mirror.

Babs was asleep against Quinn's shoulder.

Quinn was awake—staring right back at him.

"I don't know what you're talking about," he said, too quickly. "We're not dating. We're still just friends. Like we used to be."

Stephanie lowered her gaze, twisting her fingers in her lap. "You're more than friends like you used to be," she whispered.

She didn't think he would hear her over the engine and music.

But he did.

"Do you want to be friends like that?" he asked, blunt and disarming. Not teasing. Not cruel. Just... asking.

He glanced in the mirror again.

Quinn's face had gone red before she turned away.

Stephanie's cheeks flushed too, bright and quick beneath the dim dashboard glow.

Her own honesty surprised her as much as it did him. "I wanted to be a friend like that, Chris."

Chris coughed—hard enough to startle Babs awake but not enough to shake the wheel.

"What's going on?" Babs mumbled.

Stephanie didn't have time to answer. Quinn softly repeated every word of Stephanie and Chris's exchange, her voice gentle, almost protective.

When she finished, Babs leaned forward between the seats. "You go, girl."

Stephanie shot her a glare, but Babs only grinned.

Quinn flashed an "OK" sign.

Babs gave two thumbs-up.

Stephanie turned forward, face burning, just in time to see Chris watching her out of the corner of his eye.

"I think it might be too late for that to happen anymore," Stephanie murmured.

"Hmm."

Chris offered nothing more than that noncommittal sound—neither agreement nor denial, just a vague vibration that carried nowhere. Stephanie couldn't tell if it held meaning or if he simply didn't feel like granting her one.

Silence reclaimed the car. The radio filled the space where conversation should've been, but even that felt thin.

Ten quiet minutes passed before Babs finally broke. "Chris... where are we going? This is the middle of nowhere."

Quinn spoke next—surprisingly. "I haven't seen anything for a while."

Chris flicked a quick glance at his phone, the GPS glowing in his hand. "According to this, about ten more minutes. Next exit."

The girls leaned forward, watching the dark road with new attention. The car slipped off the main highway, and Chris turned right at the end of the ramp.

He had said ten minutes, but that time stretched and doubled, stretching their nerves with it.

No buildings. No signs. No turn-offs. Nothing but asphalt swallowed by the headlights.

The fog they'd driven through seemed to peel away behind them, revealing a sky that looked... wrong. The stars felt too sharp, the moon slightly misplaced—like a picture someone had hung crooked without noticing.

Stephanie stared at it too long, trying to understand why it unsettled her.

She didn't have time to find an answer.

Ahead, the sky brightened—not with sunrise, but with something far harsher.

Neon.

Electric glare spilled over the treetops like a chemical sunrise. Chris slowed the car in the middle of the empty road, not bothering to pull aside. None of them cared about blocking nonexistent traffic.

They all stared ahead.

"Is this the place?" Stephanie whispered.

"I hope not," Babs muttered, inching closer to Quinn.

Chris checked the GPS again, then his text thread with John. "He said the place is called 'Ruby's Spot.'"

Three buildings materialized out of the darkness:

A sagging motel.

A rust-bitten garage.

A bar glowing like a radioactive wound.

The garage had a sign that might once have said gas, but now read simply Gus, as if the building had taken a nickname for itself after being abandoned.

The motel was worse—its name faded almost beyond recognition. Sunshine Hills Motel.

Stephanie snorted. There hadn't been sunshine in this place since God chose the earth's color palette.

Babs laughed too, the sound shaky. Everyone in Ionia joked the region was flat enough to shame the sheriff's backside, and this bleak strip of land seemed determined to prove the comparison generous.

Then there was the bar.

"Loud" didn't describe the sound. It described the light—neon layered over neon, signs buzzing in saturated blues and reds and greens. Stephanie wondered how the electric bill hadn't sent the place into bankruptcy.

Motorcycles lined the front—enough to suggest a club was inside.

Behind them sat John's unmistakable truck.

"So... do you really think this is it?" Stephanie asked.

Chris checked his phone, then the bar again. "Yeah. This is it."

He scanned the girls' faces for objections. Nobody offered one.

He steered into the parking lot and pulled in beside John's truck.

Up close, Stephanie revised her earlier assessment.

This wasn't merely "shabby."

Calling it shabby was like calling an outhouse an ensuite bathroom.

This place wasn't run-down.

It had given up.

Stephanie had officially reached her limit. If she had her way, she'd get back in Chris's car, drive home, and shower off the feeling that she was about to contract tetanus just from looking at the place.

She couldn't imagine the inside being better.

"What exactly was John's plan? That we spend homecoming weekend in the ER?" she asked.

"Yeah, this place looks like a bag of hot dog poop," Chris muttered.

"You're being unfair to dog poop," Stephanie shot back.

Chris huffed, pulled out his phone. "I'm calling John. I'm not walking into that biohazard without proof he isn't zipped in a body bag."

Babs stepped closer to Stephanie while Chris dialed, gripping Stephanie's arm and pressing against her for warmth. Her cheerleading skirt did nothing against the cold.

Stephanie noticed Quinn was wearing a skirt about the same length as Babs's—and the torn panties flashed behind her earlier told Stephanie Quinn was probably freezing.

Or embarrassed.

Or both.

Stephanie extended her hand toward Quinn. Quinn hesitated, then accepted the gesture, stepping closer like a shy creature unsure she deserved it.

Babs gave Quinn a comforting smile, then looked at Stephanie. "I'm not sure about this, Steph."

Stephanie squeezed Quinn's hand, then patted the ones wrapped around her bicep. "Let's see what John wants. If it feels sketchy, we ask Chris or John to take us home."

"Okay," Quinn whispered.

"If you say so," Babs echoed.

The three girls fell silent, watching Chris as he finished his call.

He turned toward them with one raised brow, noticing how tightly they were clustered together. He figured it was because of the dark beyond the neon, or because the building radiated the kind of light that warned normal people to run.

"We're waiting on John," he said. "He'll be out in a minute."

Right on cue, John pushed through the bar door. "Hey! Did you enjoy the scenic drive?" he asked with too much cheer.

Chris crossed his arms. "The drive was fine. What are we doing here? And where's Henry?"

John jerked a thumb toward the bar. "Inside. Nursing a tequila shot like it's medicine."

"He's drinking?" Babs blurted.

John shrugged. "I wouldn't call it drinking. We got here after the game. He's been holding the same shot since."

Stephanie narrowed her eyes. "Did you bring us here to drink?"

John mock-fired finger-guns at her. "Ding, ding. You win a cupie doll."

Stephanie turned toward the car, ready to leave, but Babs grabbed her arm.

"You want to stay for this?" Stephanie asked gently.

Babs shook her head so hard her ponytail whipped her shoulder. "No. But I can't leave Henry in there alone. I have to check on him."

Stephanie heard the plea under her friend's words—felt it in the tremor of her hand. She exhaled, chin dropping, then lifted her head again with the resigned, soft smile Babs had been hoping for.

John darted toward the entrance, and the girls followed him.

They passed the motorcycles, stepped out of the neon glow, and approached the door. John held it open, but Chris stopped short, blocking the way.

"You still never told me why we're here," he said, his tone firm.

John raised his hands in surrender, accidentally letting the door start to close. "To drink, Chris. Relax."

He laughed, but it didn't land.

The girls slipped inside. John relinquished the door and followed.

It shut behind them with a hard clack, echoing like a warning.

They stepped into the dim bar—an airless space carved from shadow and stale smoke—and none of them had the faintest idea how this night was about to end.

Chapter Five

Stepping inside, Stephanie briefly wondered whether she'd walked into a hidden-camera prank. The place smelled like spilled beer and cigarettes that died five presidents ago. A scatter of tables sat huddled on one side of the room, each surrounded by mismatched chairs that looked like they needed tetanus shots more than the customers did. Sitting in them felt like a gamble. Standing felt smarter.

The tables formed a narrow aisle leading from the entrance to the long wooden bar at the opposite end—an unspoken warning: don't wander off the path unless you want trouble. Stephanie hoped nothing would force her to walk the full length of it.

Across from the bar, in jarring contrast to the décor, two pristine pool tables gleamed under their lights—luxury islands in a sea of neglect. Whoever owned this place apparently loved neon and billiards more than structural integrity.

Outside, the bar's exterior lights could've rivaled noon. Inside, the mood shifted to a muted dusk. It wasn't dark enough to trip over anything, but the difference felt deliberate—like stepping behind the curtain of a stage set that wasn't meant to be examined too closely.

The moment they walked in, instinct demanded they pause. Eyes adjusting, senses recalibrating, scanning for hazards. Stephanie suspected the carefully cleared aisle from the door wasn't accidental. People needed a safe way in.

Half a dozen men clustered around the pool tables, dressed in varying degrees of animal hide and denim—the kind of wardrobe that suggested the motorcycles outside belonged to them. A few more leaned against the bar, close enough to the pool tables to watch the game and the newcomers at the same time.

The atmosphere shifted when the door slammed shut behind them. Heads turned. Eyes narrowed. Conversations died. Even the battered jukebox—currently stuck on a wheezing rendition of '80s rock—gave up mid-song.

For a moment, the silence felt like a dare.

Stephanie almost opened her mouth just to break it—but Henry beat her to it.

"Hey, Steph. Chris. Over here," he called, lifting one hand in an awkward half-wave.

Relief colored his voice, and she couldn't blame him. If she'd been alone in this place waiting for friends, she'd be relieved too.

Stephanie noticed his other hand was clamped so tightly around a shot glass that she was amazed it hadn't shattered. Whatever he was feeling, it wasn't relaxation.

She strode to him, pried the glass from his fingers before he could protest, and immediately pulled him into a hug to distract him from the theft.

"Hey, Henry," she murmured.

When she stepped back, she saw Babs hovering—wanting her turn. Stephanie moved aside, and Babs slipped into Henry's arms, holding on longer than he did.

"How are you doing?" Stephanie asked once Henry disentangled himself from Babs.

Henry sighed. "I'm alright, Steph. I didn't want to be here, but John insisted. He kept talking about 'reuniting the gang' and didn't want to hear 'no.'"

John materialized behind Henry, draping an arm over his shoulders like a sloppy mantle. With his free hand, he snatched the shot glass Henry had abandoned.

He knocked it back in one gulp and slammed the empty glass onto the bar. A few bikers cheered from down the counter.

"Damn right I didn't wanna hear 'no,'" John slurred. "Been way too long since we all hung out, and I'm sick of the bullshit keeping us apart."

He waved theatrically at the bartender, who began setting out six shot glasses with the efficiency of someone who'd seen far worse nights. Stephanie watched her pour tequila without once asking for IDs.

John pointed at Chris, who'd taken a seat closer to the middle of the bar. "This is the only shot for you and Henry, man. Gotta keep the designated driver sober."

A shot glass appeared in front of Stephanie. She glanced between her friends, then at the bartender, who met her gaze with a flat, unbothered expression. Tequila bottle in one hand, dirty towel slung over her shoulder, she looked ready to refill endlessly.

The lack of ID check didn't surprise Stephanie—but the ease of it unsettled her. It made the whole place feel less like a bar and more like a hole in the universe where rules didn't apply.

John, Henry, and Babs all wore their letter jackets; Babs still had on her full cheer uniform. By contrast, Stephanie and Quinn might as well have had minor stamped on their foreheads. On a good day, Quinn barely looked fourteen. Tonight, with her nerves and that skirt, she looked twelve. None of them had any business being served anything stronger than soda—and here they were with tequila.

Babs already had her glass in hand. Chris and Quinn held theirs, ready. Only Stephanie and Henry hadn't picked up theirs yet.

When Henry finally reached for his, Stephanie gave in and followed, fingers closing around the glass. Not everyone looked eager, but there was a quiet, shared understanding: this wasn't just about drinking. It was a ritual. A line they were all choosing to cross together.

Stephanie looked at Chris. It felt natural to take her cue from him—he'd always been the center of their orbit. She gave him a small nod.

Chris lifted his glass. "To friends," he said.

The others echoed it, then tossed back the shots.

The burn hit instantly—faces twisted, throats flamed, stomachs warmed.

"Whoo, that burned real good," John crowed, planting his empty glass on the bar. He clapped his hands onto Henry's shoulders from behind, while Babs slid closer, standing in the space between Henry's knees. Henry looked like he wanted to fold in on himself.

"Congratulations to the MVP of our homecoming victory—fifty-five to zero!" John announced, hoisting one of Henry's arms in the air.

Stephanie heard something in his voice she didn't like: a thin edge of sarcasm, a flicker of heat in his eyes when Babs kissed Henry's cheek and whooped for him.

"Congratulations, Henry," Babs said, earnest and bright.

Whatever Stephanie thought she'd seen in John's face vanished so quickly she almost doubted she'd seen it at all. Then Quinn spoke up.

"How did Henry make MVP?" she asked. "I thought he was just the kicker."

"'Just' the kicker," John repeated, grinning. He mimed stiff-arming an invisible defender. "Our boy didn't score any touchdowns, but he put up thirteen points on his own."

Stephanie and Babs, who had both been at the game, still looked confused. John sighed and spelled it out.

"Two field goals, three points each, plus the extra point after all seven of our touchdowns. That's thirteen. I scored the most touchdowns and only got twelve."

The math finally landed. Everyone looked at Henry differently, and he flushed scarlet.

"Wow," Chris said. "Great job, Henry. That's pretty damn cool."

Henry ducked his head. Babs cupped his cheeks and tilted his face back up.

"I wasn't trying to get MVP," he said. "I was just doing my part. I didn't even realize until Coach said something in the locker room."

John slid between Henry and Babs to reach the bar—despite there being more than enough space on the other side. The move was deliberate. He ordered another shot, then turned back to the group.

"Yeah, well, Coach made sure we all heard. And there were scouts there tonight," he said. "I was supposed to shine. But you did good, Henry."

The bartender handed him his tequila. John threw it back and set the glass down hard.

Stephanie laid a hand on his shoulder, feeling the tension rolling off him. "You okay?" she asked quietly.

John stared at her for a heartbeat, unreadable, then shrugged her hand off and walked away. He claimed a chair at a nearby table and dropped into it, saying nothing.

An awkward silence settled until Quinn—of all people—broke it.

"Are you going to try for a football scholarship, Henry?" she asked, fingers covering her mouth as she spoke.

Henry shook his head. "That's not what I want. That was always John's dream, not mine. I don't want to take that from him."

"Don't worry about it, buddy," John called over, managing a thin smile that didn't quite reach his eyes.

Movement at the bar snagged Stephanie's attention. A woman had slid onto the stool next to Chris. She turned toward him with a syrupy drawl.

"Hiya. I'm Pinky."

Chris blinked, thrown off his axis. Up close, Pinky looked like trouble wrapped in bright lipstick and a low-cut top. Her chest did half the talking.

"Hi, Pinky," Chris managed, grinning despite himself.

Stephanie watched the grin and felt something sharp twist in her ribs. Irrational or not, she wanted to walk over and smack the back of his head just for enjoying it.

'Chris is not my boyfriend,' she reminded herself. *'He's not mine. I don't get a vote.'*

She turned back to Henry and Babs, forcing herself to focus.

At the bar, Chris rallied fast. Pinky's attention lit up something reckless in him. He held out his hand.

"I'm Chris," he said. "Can I get your number?"

Pinky's smile widened—but before she could answer, a shadow fell over them. A man even larger than John wedged himself between Pinky and Chris.

"Hey, Tank," Pinky said, instantly shifting her attention.

Tank turned his back to Chris, facing his sister. "This little boy bothering you?" he asked.

Chris snorted. "Seriously? That's the line you're going with?" He started to rise, choosing distance over drama, when Tank spoke again.

"Sit your ass down, boy," Tank said, eyes still on Pinky.

The word landed like a slap.

As a Black kid, Chris had learned to read that word in a hundred different tones. Coming from a White man—any White man—it crawled under his skin.

"Who the hell are you calling 'boy'?" he growled.

Tank pivoted to face him fully. Up close, he was worse—six feet of solid muscle, easily two-fifty. A scar carved from above his left eye to the corner of his mouth left that eye cloudy and his whole expression mean.

He looked Chris over, slow and assessing. Then he smirked.

"Oh, I see," he said. "How 'bout this: sit your narrow ass down, kid, before I put you down."

The word changed. The threat didn't.

A dozen comebacks lined up on Chris's tongue. All of them tasted like broken teeth.

He'd spent years learning how to take a punch—from a drunk man in boxing gloves who called it "training." He knew how to fight. He also knew what a losing fight looked like.

Every bit of that hard-earned survival instinct whispered the same thing: Sit. Down.

So he did. He let gravity pull him back onto the barstool. It was, he admitted to himself, the smartest thing he'd done in a long time.

Didn't stop it from feeling like someone had reached in and scooped out what was left of his pride.

Humiliation pressed down heavy. It wasn't just Tank. It was his father. It was every "boy" and every shove back into his place. It was the reminder that strength made the rules, took what it wanted, hurt who it pleased, and then wrote the story afterward to make it all sound justified.

History belonged to people like Tank. People like his father. People who didn't have to swallow words to keep their teeth.

The thought hollowed him out. Hope thinned.

And then glass shattered.

For a heartbeat, Chris thought it was just another bottle breaking somewhere behind the bar. Then he saw it—saw the jagged neck of a broken bottle drive into Tank's throat. Saw John's eyes, wild and bright, as he twisted.

Blood fountained.

The bar erupted. Screams, chairs scraping, the crash of bodies and panic all hit at once, and the world dissolved into chaos.

Chapter Six

"What the fuck, man?" Chris's scream cut through the bar as he kicked a stool out of his way, almost tripping over it in his scramble to get away from Tank.

Tank hit the floor hard, hands clamped over his throat. Blood poured between his fingers. The realization of what had just happened spread through the room like shockwave—shouts, curses, chair legs scraping, someone yelling for help and no one moving.

Stephanie heard the screaming before she realized some of it was hers. Quinn's and Babs's voices tangled with hers, high and sharp. Henry lurched to his feet behind them, craning over Babs's shoulder to see past Stephanie.

The moment he saw Tank on the floor, something in him snapped into place. Henry wrapped his arms around Babs and hauled her back, shielding her, guiding her away from the spreading pool of red. Quinn just stood there, hands clamped to her temples, fingers twisted in her hair, eyes huge and unblinking.

"What the hell did you do, John?" Chris shouted.

He wasn't really asking. Everybody knew what John had done. There was a man bleeding out on the floor with a broken bottle in his neck. The words were just Chris's panic trying to grab onto something.

Then he moved.

He grabbed Quinn by the arm and shoved her toward the door. She tried to look back at Tank, the words tumbling out of her mouth in a trembling loop. "Oh my God, oh my God, oh my God—"

"Keep moving. Don't stop," Chris barked.

He snatched Stephanie's hand next and yanked her after him. One quick glance over his shoulder showed Henry still frozen, clutching Babs like she might disappear if he let go.

"Let's move, Henry!" Chris yelled.

Stephanie stumbled, finally catching up to his urgency as his grip dragged her along. Chris shoved Quinn toward the entrance and risked another look back.

Henry was still rooted.

"Now!" Chris roared.

That did it. Henry jerked into motion, half-dragging Babs with him. As the door loomed, another figure barreled out of the chaos—John, face white, eyes wild, blood spatter on his sleeves. He burst through the gap behind them, nearly slamming into Chris's back as they all shoved their way outside.

Getting out took seconds. No one stopped to wonder why it had felt so much longer coming in.

Cold air slapped them the second they hit the parking lot. Chris drove them across the gravel at a dead run, eyes skimming the shadows for his car.

When they reached it, he cursed the lack of a key fob for the first time in his life. A newer car would've unlocked itself. Instead, he was elbow-deep in metal teeth and panic.

"Come on, come on, come on," he muttered, fingers fumbling from key to key.

Henry kept one arm squashed around Babs and his eyes on the bar's door. "Hurry up, man," he urged, voice cracking.

Babs pressed herself so tightly against Henry's chest it looked like she was trying to climb inside him. Stephanie hovered by the driver's door, glancing from Chris's hands to the entrance and back again.

"Why's this taking so damn long?" she demanded, voice pitched high with adrenaline.

"I'm moving as fast as I can," Chris snapped.

Finally, his fingers found the right shape. He jammed the key into the lock without bending it or gouging the paint—not that he cared about either right now. The only victory that mattered was getting the hell away from here.

"Get in," he barked.

Stephanie dove across the seat to hit the unlock button on the inside. Henry yanked the front passenger seat forward to make room.

"Go, go," he urged.

Babs scrambled into the back first, Quinn right behind her, both of them shaking. Henry climbed in last, dragging the seat back into place and slamming the door.

Chris cursed his beautiful, stupid two-door for the second time. A four-door and they'd have been in the car thirty seconds ago.

He twisted the key in the ignition. The engine roared awake. He dropped the transmission into gear and stomped the accelerator. The rear tires spun on the loose gravel before finally biting, spraying stones in a rooster tail behind them as he wrestled the wheel and shot for the asphalt.

They tore down the empty road the way they'd come in, the speedometer climbing well past the limit. The car shuddered as the tires howled over the worn blacktop.

Stephanie's breath came in ragged gasps. She kept twisting in her seat to stare through the rear window, waiting for headlights to appear—bikes, trucks, cruiser lights, something. It felt wrong that nothing was there. Wrong, and worse: temporary. Like the danger hadn't been avoided, just delayed, waiting around the next bend.

The noise inside the car rose fast—panicked questions, half-sobbed curses, Babs crying, Quinn whispering prayers. It all slammed together until it was just one shrill roar in Stephanie's skull.

"Shut the hell up, everyone!" she screamed.

Silence dropped like a curtain. Only the engine and the rush of air against the car kept screaming.

She swallowed, forced her voice into something sharper, more controlled. "What the flying fuck was that, Henry?"

He didn't hesitate. "How the hell should I know, Steph?" he shot back. He understood exactly what she meant. None of them knew what they'd just been pulled into.

Stephanie twisted toward the front again. "Chris, do you have any idea what just happened back there?"

He kept his eyes glued to the road, knuckles pale on the wheel. "I don't have a damn clue," he said. "Why don't you ask John?"

He jerked his thumb toward the backseat.

Stephanie decided to take him up on it. "John—" she began, turning toward the rear.

The rest of the sentence died in her throat. She twisted farther, trying to get a full view of the back seat. Babs. Quinn. An empty corner.

She blinked, then turned back to Chris. "Where's John?"

Her voice stayed level, but the confusion bled through.

For the first time since they'd pulled out of the parking lot, Chris risked a proper look at her. He could tell from her face this wasn't just panic noise. "Ain't he in the back?" he asked flatly.

Stephanie shook her head, the calm cracking. "He's not here, Chris. What part didn't you understand?"

"Damn it," Chris hissed. "Did anyone see him before we left?"

Silence answered him. Just the engine, the tires, and Babs and Quinn's muffled sobs.

Stephanie wet her lips. "Are we going back to get him?"

Chris stared at the road, the answer coming too fast. "Hell no."

Though John had unquestionably triggered their current nightmare, Stephanie still saw him as their friend—one of theirs. "I think we should go back, Chris," she said, keeping her tone as even as she could.

He shook his head hard. "There is no way in hell I'm turning this car around and going back there."

Henry spoke up from the back, adjusting his hold on Babs, pulling her closer. "Even if we do go back, there's not much we can do for him now," he said quietly.

"We can at least be there when the police arrive," Stephanie argued.

Chris scoffed, a shiver running up his spine at the memory of the bottle and the blood. "And why should we? He's the crazy bastard who stabbed that guy in the neck with a broken bottle. Or did you forget that part?" His jaw clenched. He didn't bother to look at Stephanie's glare.

"It looked to me like John did that to keep that guy from beating your ass," Stephanie shot back.

Chris let out a long breath and eased off the gas. The adrenaline spike had burned off; now survival instincts wanted more control. The high beams cut into the dark, but the night felt too thick, like it was swallowing light whole.

"Fine," he said. "I'm not going back, and that's final. But we can call the cops and tell them what we saw. They'll get there. He won't be alone."

It was the closest thing to a compromise he could stomach. He wasn't going to walk back into a murder scene, but he also wasn't ready to pretend John didn't exist.

Stephanie didn't like it, but she took what she could get. She dug her phone out of her pocket—and froze.

The screen was black.

That wasn't possible. It had been on half-battery earlier. She jabbed the power button. Nothing. No glow, no logo. Dead.

"My phone's dead," she said slowly. "Henry, can I use yours?"

He nudged Babs gently so she'd sit up enough for him to reach into his pocket. He pulled his phone out, thumbed the screen. Nothing. "That's weird. Mine's dead too," he said, genuinely confused.

That sent both girls in the backseat scrambling. Babs and Quinn dug out their phones, holding up their own dead screens like proof.

Stephanie turned forward again just as she felt the car start to slow. For a second, she thought they'd finally reached the on-ramp to the state road.

Then she saw the light.

"What the fuck?" Chris said, more statement than question. "What the actual fuck?"

Stephanie leaned forward, peering through the windshield. Neon glared back at her, too familiar. "I thought you said you weren't coming back here," she said carefully.

"I wasn't trying to come back here," Chris ground out through his teeth.

"Did you... somehow turn us around?" Quinn asked, fingers digging into the back of Stephanie's seat as she leaned between them, eyes wide.

Chris shoved his foot down, gunning the car past the bar in the same direction they'd taken when they first left it. "No. I did not turn this car around," he snapped. "We were going straight. No side roads, no driveways, no turnoffs. There is no way I turned us around without noticing."

Stephanie stared out her window. The dark trees whipped by, unbroken. "Could we have missed the turnoff and turned ourselves around in the dark somehow?" she asked, hating how thin it sounded even as she said it.

Chris shot her a quick, sharp look. "We were going straight, Stephanie," he repeated. "There was nowhere to go."

Henry leaned forward between the seats, his calm voice cutting through the rising panic. "Let's not dwell on that right now. It doesn't matter how it happened. Just keep going. We'll all watch for the turn."

Chris and Stephanie both nodded. It was something to do, at least.

They drove in tense silence for several more miles. Stephanie kept Chris's phone face up in her lap, watching the "No Service" icon stare back at her like it was mocking them.

"Chris," she said softly, "let me see your phone."

"It's in my jacket pocket," he said, not taking his eyes off the road.

She fished it out, almost sagged in relief when the screen lit. At least something worked. "It's not dead, thank God," she said. Then her shoulders slumped. "But you've got no connection."

"Keep an eye on it," he said. "Maybe we'll pick up a signal farther on."

So she watched. The little empty bars stayed empty, and her leg bounced in rhythm with the car's speed.

After a while, Henry leaned forward again. "Any luck?"

"Nope. Not yet," Stephanie said.

"Don't you think we've driven too far?" he asked Chris.

"Yeah," Chris admitted. "We should've hit the state road a while back." He squinted through the windshield. "There's a brightening up ahead. See it, over the trees? Might be lights from the next exit."

Stephanie looked up, tracking the glow above the treeline. Her stomach sank. "That can't be our turn," she said quietly. "The state road didn't have lights like that."

"We'll find out soon enough," Chris muttered.

A few minutes later, they did.

Chris eased the car to a stop in the middle of the road. Out here, with nothing but woods and blacktop, it didn't feel like a risk. There would be plenty of time to move if anyone else appeared.

All five of them stared out the driver's side window.

Same abandoned service garage. Same sagging motel. Same neon-drenched sign: Ruby's Place.

Chris looked at Stephanie, his eyes hollow with confusion. "I didn't turn. The road didn't turn," he said. His gaze slid back to the bar's blazing lights. "How?"

"There's no way," Stephanie whispered.

Babs started sobbing again, soft and hopeless. Henry wrapped his arm around her shoulders, pulling her into his side.

"Guys, what is this?" Quinn asked, voice shaking. "What's happening?"

"I don't know," Stephanie said. She glanced at the phone in her hand—still no signal—then at Chris. Whatever questions she had were mirrored in his face.

"What do we do now?" Chris asked her.

That threw her.

There'd never been an official leader. No one had voted. If anyone filled that role, it was him. When Chris was around, the group worked. When he wasn't, everything frayed. Now he was looking at her like she had the answers.

She looked from face to face: Babs, Quinn, Henry. All of them staring at her, hope and fear mixed together like she was supposed to fix this.

"I don't know what to do," she snapped. "I didn't plan this debacle!"

She was about to keep going when something outside caught her eye. She leaned to the side, peering past Chris out the driver's window.

Chris noticed the shift and turned his head. He followed her line of sight—and froze.

John stood beside the car, waving at them like they'd just pulled into his driveway twenty minutes late.

Chris looked back at Stephanie. She just shrugged, bewildered. If anything, John's appearance made the whole night feel even less real.

"Roll the window down and ask him what's going on," she said.

"What are you talking about? We shouldn't even be here," Chris shot back.

She didn't answer. Just stared at him until he turned back to the glass. With a reluctant sigh, he hit the button. The window slid down.

"Hey, where have you guys been?" John grinned. "Henry and I have been waiting for you forever."

Chris stared at him. "What are you talking about? We've already been here, and Henry's with us."

John leaned in, resting his forearms on the door as he scanned the car's interior. His brows knit. "He is? I thought I left him inside. Where is he?"

"Right there—" Chris started, turning to point.

The rest of the sentence died. Stephanie, Babs, and Quinn all turned with him.

Babs let out a tiny, terrified sound when she saw the empty space beside her.

Henry's seat was vacant.

"Quit joking, guys," John called, tone light, oblivious. "Hurry up and park and come inside. Henry and I will see you when you get in."

He pushed away from the car and jogged toward the bar's entrance, leaving the four of them staring after him.

"This is crazy," Stephanie said, voice shaking now. "Henry was just in the car with us. He was right there." She pointed at the empty corner. "We left here twice and ended up back here both times when we shouldn't have."

Chris didn't argue. Strangeness hung thick in the air, undeniable now.

He turned the wheel and eased the car onto the cracked concrete of the parking lot, pulling up next to John's truck. The subtle change from gravel to slab went unnoticed. Compared to everything else, it was nothing.

"Let's go," Chris said after killing the engine. "We're going inside to find out what the hell is going on."

Chapter Seven

Chris didn't just walk back into the bar—he hit the doors like a storm front.

Stephanie could practically see the chip on his shoulder jutting out in front of him, sharp and daring someone to take a swipe. If one of the bikers so much as breathed wrong, she had no doubt Chris would swing at him.

She braced herself for what she expected to see: Tank sprawled on the floor. Blood everywhere. The shattered bottle still wedged in his throat.

Instead—

Nothing.

No body. No blood pool. No paramedics. No cops. No screaming.

Just the bar. Just people. Just... wrong.

Quinn and Babs clung to Stephanie's arms, their confusion matching the cold knot in her stomach. Something that huge, that violent, didn't just... disappear. But Chris was too pissed to notice the absence. His anger had locked onto the only familiar sight in the room.

Henry.

He sat at the bar exactly as before, gripping a full shot of tequila so tightly his knuckles had gone white.

"Hey, Steph," Henry called, his voice echoing the same greeting from earlier like the last ninety minutes had never happened.

Stephanie opened her mouth to answer, but Chris was already at his side.

"What the hell is going on here?" Chris hissed through clenched teeth.

Henry blinked at him, genuinely puzzled, as if Chris had just asked why chairs had legs.

He didn't get a chance to answer. John slid in behind him, draping an arm over Henry's shoulders and flashing Chris a lazy smile. He reached around, took Henry's shot—and instead of tossing it back like before, he lifted it halfway, hesitated, then set it right back into Henry's stiff fingers.

"Isn't it obvious what's happening here, Chris?" John said. "We're..." His voice drifted off. He frowned up at the ceiling like the words might be written there. Rubbed his scalp. Worked his jaw. Finally, he settled on: "We're just having a drink, buddy."

Stephanie swayed.

The room tilted, edges blurring. Her stomach rolled. Quinn and Babs grabbed her just in time and steered her onto a barstool before she went down.

This was the same moment. The same greeting. The same pose. But it wasn't. She'd already lived this.

A sharp squeak ripped out of Babs. Stephanie followed her gaze—and felt her skin crawl.

Tank.

He strolled up to the bar as if nothing had ever touched him harder than a barstool. He ordered a beer. Turned, leered toward Babs. The scar slashed across his face. His cloudy eye. His whole throat. Intact.

He should have been dead on this floor. Instead, he lifted his bottle, took a drink, breathed.

Chris turned at Babs's noise and froze. For one second he looked like someone had just pulled the bones out of his legs.

Tank stared back at him, unmoved.

No hole in his neck. No blood. No broken bottle. Alive.

Chris's gaze skittered away like it had touched a hot stove. He spun back toward Stephanie. Her face had gone even paler, and her fingers dug into his sleeve like a lifeline.

He moved in beside her, grateful for the excuse to anchor himself to something that wasn't bending reality under his feet.

Quinn and Babs drifted toward Henry and John, gravitating to them for comfort. Stephanie didn't move. When Chris stepped closer, she latched onto his arm and held on.

"This is insane, Chris," she whispered. "That man was stabbed with a bottle. What's happening?"

"I don't know my damn self," he whispered back. "I'm just as confused as you. Your guess is as good as mine. A lot of strange shit's gone down since we got here."

She didn't dare look at Tank again. It felt wrong to see a man stand who'd already bled out in front of her. The only way that made sense was if someone had staged the whole thing—and she knew they hadn't. All she had to do was look at Chris's shirt.

"Chris," she said, pointing. "That guy should be dead. You still have his blood on you."

Dark droplets flecked his shirt in a diagonal spray. Arterial. Real.

"And the bottle," she added, nodding toward a nearby table.

A jagged brown bottle lay on its side like a centerpiece that didn't belong. Blood still clung to the glass. As they watched, Karen the bartender came over with a broom and dustpan, sweeping up the scattered shards around the table. She picked up the main piece with bare hands, unbothered by the dried red smeared along the rim.

Chris watched her work, his mouth pressed into a hard line. When she walked away with the dustpan, he looked back at Stephanie. Her pulse beat frantic and visible at the side of her neck.

"Henry was in that car with us," she said slowly. "I know I didn't imagine that."

"If you imagined it, it was a shared hallucination," Chris said. "Quinn, Babs, and I saw him there too."

"There is something way crazy going on here," she said, voice starting to shake. "Is this some kind of weird television prank show?"

Chris shook his head. "I'm with you on 'batshit crazy,' but it's no TV show." He tugged his shirt away from his chest, examining the blood. It wasn't corn syrup. It wasn't staged. "We left here. We should be miles away from this mess."

Behind the bar, Karen dumped the glass and went back to polishing bottles. On the far side, Tank leaned in to say something to her, then walked off toward the pool tables with his fresh beer.

"Karen," he called over his shoulder, "send another round of beers over."

His voice scraped down Chris's spine. Hearing it again felt worse than watching him drop the first time.

Before they could process that, Karen was back in front of them, setting down a tray of fresh tequila shots. Beer for the bikers. Tequila for the kids.

Six glasses hit the bar.

Their friends all stared at the shots with variations of confusion, dread, and temptation—except John and Henry. John already looked comfortably pickled. Henry just clung to his glass like it was the last solid object in a sinking world.

Quinn, though, focused on a simpler question: who the hell had ordered tequila again?

She caught Stephanie's eye. Stephanie gave her a tiny, helpless smile that meant absolutely nothing and everything at once.

Quinn decided gratitude didn't matter. Nerves did.

She grabbed the nearest shot and downed it in one go.

The burn hit. She slapped the empty glass down, raised her hand to Karen, and watched the refill with hungry focus. By the time she'd knocked back the second, the others started to move, each grabbing their own shot and swallowing the burn like medicine.

John planted himself between the two halves of their group—Chris and Stephanie to his right, Henry and the girls to his left. He threw back two more shots in quick succession, then surfaced with a gasp.

"Damn," he said, grinning. "Those hit the spot."

"Are you alright, John?" Stephanie asked. She wasn't asking about the tequila.

For a moment, his eyes wouldn't quite land. He rubbed them, blinked, then finally got them to focus on her.

"I'mma lil' tipsy," he slurred. "Had a good night, tho."

Another mysterious shot had appeared in his hand. Stephanie shot Karen a glare, but the bartender just kept working—pouring drinks, wiping the bar, feeding the machine.

John staggered sideways until he reached Henry again. He slung an arm over Henry's shoulders, leaning heavily.

"This shot's for da most valuable player of da evenin'," he announced, lifting the glass and sweeping his gaze over them. "He scored—"

"Thirteen points during the game," Chris cut in without thinking.

John blinked at him. The coach had only announced that in the locker room. Chris hadn't been there. John opened his mouth to ask how he knew, then decided it didn't matter.

"My man here is da top scorer and ever'one's hero," John said instead.

The tone didn't match the words.

He turned back to Henry and, without warning, leaned in and kissed him full on the mouth.

Henry jolted like he'd been shocked. He shoved John hard. John stumbled backwards and landed on the floor, laughing.

"What the fuck, dude?" Henry snapped.

He scrubbed his sleeve across his mouth like he could wipe away both taste and memory. Chris stepped forward and offered a hand, but John jerked his arm away and pushed himself upright on his own.

"Leave me—" John started, then cut himself off and turned away.

He shouldered past Henry, returning to the bar and bracing his elbows on the wood. Chris followed and came to stand beside him.

"What's going on with you, man?" Chris asked low. "You're acting out of pocket. We need to keep our heads. Stephanie and I have noticed some really weird shit tonight. I wanted to talk to you and Henry about it."

John hunched forward, burying his face in his hands. His voice dropped to a hoarse whisper.

"Chris, I think I'm losin' my mind," he said. "Feels like I've been trapped in this damn place for weeks, and I can't get out. You and the girls show up, and it starts all over again."

"What are you talking about?" Chris asked, leaning closer.

John lifted his head. "Every time I drive away from here, I end up right back where I started."

Chris's breath hitched.

That was exactly what had just happened to them.

While Chris tried to process that, Stephanie touched Henry's shoulder, drawing his attention away from John and Chris. When he turned, she searched his face, looking past the surface.

"Henry," she said quietly, "why do you tolerate the way John treats you? He's become a bully."

He shifted, eyes sliding away. "I don't know what you're talking about, Steph." He pushed his glasses up the bridge of his nose.

She knew that tell. He'd had it since they were kids.

"You know exactly what I'm talking about," she said. "He's been bullying you and treating you like shit for years."

Henry sighed. "He's always been jealous that Babs likes me instead of him. He's real fond of her. Tries to get her attention, but she ignores him."

"So that's a reason to let him treat you like shit?" Stephanie asked, sarcasm sharp.

"It's not like that, Steph," Henry said, adjusting his glasses again. "He's just trying to figure out how to win Babs over."

"You're lying to me," she said, eyes narrowing. "Why are you lying?"

"I'm caught in the middle, Stephanie," Henry said, voice breaking on her full name. "Things... are complicated with him right now."

The pause said more than the words.

Stephanie stepped a little closer, lowering her voice so Quinn and Babs wouldn't catch every detail. "Are you deceiving yourself," she asked, "or are you still trying to deceive me?"

He turned his face away. "Can't you just let it go, Stephanie?"

"You're holding back," she said. "You know I'd let it go if it weren't eating at you."

"How do you know something's bothering me?" Henry asked, irritated.

She almost laughed. "We've been friends longer than anybody else in this group. You've only ever called me 'Stephanie' once—first day we met. It's been 'Steph' ever since. But in the last few minutes, you've called me 'Stephanie' three times."

He met her gaze, frustration raw. "Why are you so insistent on knowing? There's nothing you can do to make this easier," he said, gesturing between himself and John. "This has been broken too long to fix that easy. Things are complicated."

Her shoulders sagged. "I thought we were friends, Henry. Friends share and support each other when they're in need."

"If I wanted help, I would've asked for it, Steph," he shot back. "Can't you see I don't need you meddling in my affairs?"

Anger rose in her chest like steam. "John's been bullying you since sophomore year—"

"You don't know what the hell you're talking about, Stephanie. Just fucking drop it," Henry snapped, louder than he intended.

She put her hands up, backing off a step, accidentally shoving him in the chest as he leaned toward her. Heads turned. For a quiet kid, Henry's outburst rang loud.

Stephanie, Babs, and Quinn all stared at him. This wasn't like him. At all.

Whatever lay between Henry and John went deeper than jealousy and football. And Henry clearly wasn't ready to expose it.

Chris looked over just as Stephanie stepped back from Henry. "Are you guys fighting now?" he asked, dread creeping in. "This place is making us act stupid. We need to get out of here. Now."

Before he could say more, John grabbed his shoulders from behind and spun him around.

"Don'tcha get it, man?" John said, eyes unfocused but strangely clear in their misery. "We're never gettin' outta here. Dis place is a black hole that's sucked us all in."

Chris stared at him. Then anger flared again, hot enough to burn through the fear.

"I don't know what's wrong with you," he said, brushing John's hands away. "I'm getting out of this madness. I don't know what's real anymore dealing with this place, but I'm getting my black ass on before I completely lose my mind like you. If you guys wanna sit around losing your minds, you can go ahead and do that."

Karen appeared at their section of the bar, planting her hands firmly on the scarred wood.

"I don't know what kinda drugs you and your friends are on," she said, looking right at Chris, "but I don't want no trouble here. If your friend's gonna overdose, take him outside. I got enough shit from them over there." She jerked her thumb at the bikers.

Chris's face twisted. "Lady, I don't wanna be here anymore," he said through his teeth. "I wish we could leave, but every time we drive off, we end up coming back to this shitty bar."

He was breathing hard now. Shoulders tight. Fists clenched.

Stephanie touched his arm again, trying to ground him.

Before he could turn fully toward her, he felt another presence at his back. He didn't need to look. The mirror behind the bar showed him everything: Tank and another big man with him, closing in.

Chris's stomach dropped. The same shrinking sensation he'd felt earlier crept under his skin. Sweat pricked his forehead. He fought the urge to wipe it away.

"Karen, is this kid getting on your nerves?" Tank rasped. "'Cause he's starting to bug the hell outta me."

"Just let it go, Tank," Karen said. "You and your brother Romeo can go back and raise hell over at the pool tables."

Tank clearly wanted to argue, maybe pick another fight just to have an excuse to hurt someone. But Karen's stare was flat and dangerous, and he knew exactly what she kept behind the bar.

He settled for glowering at Chris's back instead. With a look to Romeo, he backed off and they relocated a few stools down.

A shiver ran through Chris. He peeled himself away from the bar and walked over to the table where John had ended up again, shoulders slumped.

Whatever fire he'd had left sputtered in the stale air.

Tension had soaked into everything—the floor, the wood, the neon hum. Stephanie felt it too. Quinn and Babs hovered close, uneasily quiet. The bikers watched without openly watching. The whole bar felt like it was holding its breath.

Then the door opened.

A young man stepped inside, early to mid-twenties, nothing remarkable at first glance. Dark hair fell into his eyes no matter how often he pushed it back. Faded jeans. Scuffed boots. Black leather jacket over an off-white button-down that had seen better days.

He paused just inside the door, taking in the room with one slow sweep of his gaze. Not startled. Not confused. Just... measuring.

Then he chose a table halfway between the bar and the entrance and sat down alone, back to the wall, eyes open.

Stephanie felt all the hairs on her arms stand up.

Something had just changed. She didn't know what. But whatever rules this place had been following, they'd just made room for one more piece on the board.

.

Chapter Eight

Stephanie's eyes stayed locked on the stranger who had taken a seat at a small table near the entrance. He didn't seem interested in either group at the bar—neither the cluster of bikers by the pool tables nor her own friends huddled near Henry. Instead, he quietly studied the folded drink list set between the salt shaker and the napkin dispenser, as though it contained more urgent information than anything happening around him.

Nothing about him should have stood out. He wasn't tall, or imposing, or especially handsome. He was... ordinary. That was the unsettling part. Something about him held her attention the way the calm in a horror movie does—the quiet that comes right before the wrong thing happens.

She forced herself to look away when sudden movement beside her caught her attention.

Henry had shifted closer to Babs, trying to block Tank and Romeo's lingering stares. Both men were still watching her, openly and without shame. Babs—with her bare legs exposed in the cheer uniform and no joggers to cover them—kept tugging at her skirt, pulling it down, folding her arms, rearranging herself in her seat, doing anything she could to escape the feeling of being hunted.

"I'm sorry," Henry murmured. "This is the best I can do."

He'd positioned himself squarely between her and their stares, and for the moment, it eased the tension in Babs's shoulders. Stephanie gave him a grateful look before turning to Quinn—who had moved in close enough to grip her arm.

"What's wrong?" Stephanie whispered, careful not to attract any attention.

Quinn shifted in place, rocking from foot to foot. It almost looked like she was dancing, except nothing about her expression suggested anything close to fun. She leaned in until her breath brushed Stephanie's shoulder.

"I need to use the restroom," she whispered, voice strained with embarrassment.

Stephanie immediately understood why she'd come to her. Nobody should wander around this bar alone—not tonight, not after everything that had already happened.

She approached Karen and quietly asked where the restroom was. Karen pointed toward a dim corridor near the pool tables. Even from here, Stephanie could barely make out the women's restroom sign hanging crookedly over the door.

"Thank you," Stephanie said, before turning back to Henry and Babs.

"We'll be right back," Stephanie said softly. "Stay put, and stay together."

Babs met her eyes—checking if Stephanie wanted her to come along. Stephanie subtly shook her head. Babs nodded. Henry nodded. Everything was understood.

Stephanie and Quinn slipped through the gathered bikers, weaving between them with deliberate speed. They entered the narrow hallway and hurried toward the restroom.

Stephanie held the door open, ushering Quinn inside first. As she stepped in after her, she glanced back over her shoulder. The bar was still intact. Her friends were still there. The stranger still sat alone, studying his menu. Nothing had vanished. No one had disappeared.

For now.

Once inside, Stephanie allowed herself a breath she hadn't realized she'd been holding.

They finished quickly and met again at the sinks. Quinn's voice was barely a whisper.

"What are we still doing here? What do you think we should do?" She asked it like someone afraid the empty room might be listening.

Stephanie turned off the running faucet and planted her palms on either side of the sink.

"I don't know," she admitted. "All I know is that everything we experienced tonight shouldn't be possible. John said he's been through it too. Something is wrong with this place."

Quinn stared at her reflection, then at her hands, then at Stephanie.

"I want to leave," she said quietly. "I think we should get Chris and just... try again."

"I'm with you." Stephanie nodded. "As soon as we walk back out there, we're getting Chris, we're getting Babs, and if we can convince John and Henry, we get them too. Then we're back in the car, and we keep trying until we're out of this nightmare."

A loose strand of Quinn's hair had slipped from her scrunchie. Stephanie gently tucked it behind her ear.

"This isn't going to go on forever," Stephanie said firmly. "There has to be a way home."

Quinn managed a small, shaky smile. "We'll find it," she whispered. "Together."

"We will," Stephanie said, pulling her into a hug. "I'm not staying in this hellhole a second longer than we have to. If Chris won't leave, I'll take his keys. And if that doesn't work?"

She tightened her hold around Quinn.

"Then we walk."

Since they'd arrived at Ruby's, the night had been sliding off the rails. One impossible thing after another, each stranger than the last.

As Stephanie held Quinn, she tried to line the pieces up in her head.

Tank shouldn't be alive. No one takes a broken bottle to the neck and orders a beer afterward like it was nothing. They shouldn't have been able to drive in a straight line and end up back at the bar—twice. Henry shouldn't have vanished out of the back seat without a door opening or a window rolling down, only to be sitting exactly where they'd found him the first time they walked in.

None of it fit. None of it could be true. And yet, here they were.

She wanted answers as badly as anyone else—maybe more—but underneath that, deeper and louder, she wanted out. She wanted the night to roll itself back up and disappear. She wanted the bar gone, the blood gone, the loops undone, the wrongness erased.

Her life had been messy, sure, but it had been hers. This? This felt like someone had reached in and knocked over every carefully stacked piece just to see what fell.

And all because one of her friends decided they needed to "get the gang back together" with tequila as glue.

Stephanie slowly eased Quinn out of the hug. Something fragile and old had shifted between them. The distance of the last few years didn't feel quite as wide anymore—like the bridge they used to have was still there under the rust and dust, waiting to be walked on again.

Quinn sniffed and swiped at her eyes. Stephanie snatched a paper towel, dampened it slightly, and gently dabbed at the streaks on her friend's cheeks. The mascara smeared anyway.

"Great," Stephanie muttered. "Now we both look like we lost a fight."

Quinn glanced at the mirror, snorted, and then, unexpectedly, laughed. Stephanie's own reflection stared back at her—eyes red, eyeliner smudged, hair slightly wild.

"You look a mess, girl," Quinn said.

Stephanie let the laugh out this time. The sound shook some of the tightness out of her shoulders. "Pot, meet kettle," she shot back, lightly tapping Quinn's shoulder.

They took a few seconds to breathe. Just enough time to put their faces back together as best they could and brace themselves for whatever waited outside.

Stephanie pulled the door open and motioned for Quinn to go first.

They stepped out into hell.

The bar they had left behind barely existed anymore.

Tables were overturned or missing entirely. Sections of the wooden floor had been ripped open, jagged holes gaping like wounds. Parts of the walls were gone, blown out or torn down. What remained was splintered, blackened, or hanging crooked. Small fires smoldered along broken beams and scattered debris, flickering like candles at a wake.

Most of the roof was simply... not there.

Smoke stung Stephanie's eyes and burned her throat. Heat licked at her face. She had to fight the urge to blink and look again—like this was a trick of the light, a hallucination, a bad cut in a film.

It wasn't.

The air tasted like burnt wood and ash. Every breath dragged in the bitter tang of something ruined.

Wyrmwood and rot, she thought.

It wasn't the plant that came to mind. It was the word from Sunday-school sermons and late-night Bible stories, the one that meant bitterness and ruin and judgment. This place felt like that—like somebody had poured something poisonous over it and let it soak.

Her eyes kept climbing, drawn upward.

When they'd arrived at Ruby's, it had been just an ordinary night—the kind of black sky she'd grown up under. Now, through the shattered roofline and broken walls, the sky glowed an unnatural, sickly orange-red. It wasn't sunset. It wasn't dawn. It was the color of warm blood, thinly spread and lit from behind.

Thick clouds—wrong clouds, too dark, too heavy—boiled across that sky. They weren't storm clouds. They looked like smoke given shape, churning slowly, like something underneath was breathing.

Sweat slid down Stephanie's spine even though the air wasn't that hot. Her knees wobbled. For a second, she thought they might go out from under her.

The smell changed, deepening, thickening. Not just char and smoke now, but something harsher—sulfur, acrid and sharp. Brimstone, her brain supplied, dragging the word up from the same place as wyrmwood. Fire and brimstone. Warnings and punishments. Places you didn't come back from.

She gagged and clapped a hand over her mouth and nose. It didn't help. The stench seemed to seep around her fingers, slide down her tongue, settle in the back of her throat.

Stephanie stared, unable to make the scene resolve into anything that made sense. A few minutes ago, Ruby's had been intact—ugly and unsettling, yes, but still a bar with a roof and four walls. Now it looked like it had been gutted by something that didn't care what it broke, only that it broke enough.

Her mind tried to reject it, tried to shove the sight into some corner labeled dream or stress or panic attack. But the heat on her skin, the smoke in her lungs, the grit under her shoes all insisted the same thing:

This was real.

Something had taken whatever strange rules governed this place and twisted them even further.

And they were standing in the middle of it.

The stench hit her first—thick, blistering, chemical rot that burned as she breathed it. Heat rolled over her skin in punishing waves. But it was the sound—the shrieking, wailing, wrenching sound—that almost drove her to her knees. It felt like the air itself was peeling her open.

Stephanie's certainty snapped into place. She wasn't imagining this. Quinn felt it too—she saw it in the way Quinn's face pinched, in the panic trembling through her shoulders. Whatever this place was, they were in it together. And they were not alone.

Beyond the shattered ribs of the bar's walls, something moved. Many somethings.

Shapes writhed through the smoke and blood-colored light. Twisted silhouettes clung to one another in motions that didn't look human—some convulsing in strange, intimate tangles, others crouched low, feeding on whatever they could sink their teeth into. The ground churned with bodies locked in a grotesque rhythm, a parody of life, a parody of desire, all of it wrong.

One pair was entwined as if lost in fevered passion—until another creature tore into them, ripping flesh away with greedy, slurping bites. The victims didn't even scream. Everything out there felt like a ritual of corruption, a celebration of filth.

Every instinct Stephanie had screamed one thing: Do not let them see you.

Even breathing too loudly seemed dangerous.

She took a single step back—and bumped into the restroom door behind her. The touch of it jolted her with sudden clarity:

The door was still there.

Still open.

Still leading back into the restroom that should not, by any sane rule of the world, still exist behind a doorframe that had been blown apart.

It shouldn't be possible—but it was. And right now, it was the only thing in this nightmare that offered hope.

Her gaze flicked left and right. On either side of the door lay only the blasted wasteland stretching outward into the red sky. But through the doorway? Tile. Fluorescent light. A sink. Their world.

Quinn was only a step ahead, close enough to grab. Close enough to save.

Stephanie only had to reach out. Take her hand. Drag her back into the hallway. Back to the others. Back to sanity.

But her body refused to move. Terror locked her limbs in place. Her hand hovered uselessly at her side, fingers half-curled, as if her own survival instinct had been overridden by something colder and heavier: the fear of reaching too slowly, too late, and condemning Quinn in the process.

Her heart hammered so hard it shook her vision.

And then Quinn inhaled.

A sharp, high, sucking breath—the kind that precedes a scream.

Stephanie's body moved before her mind caught up.

Her hand snapped forward, closing around Quinn's arm just as the first note of the scream left her throat.

Too late to stay unnoticed.

Not too late to run.

Shapes surged toward them—fast, faster than she had imagined anything could move. Stephanie didn't dare look directly at them. She didn't need to. She felt the ground vibration under their approach, felt the air splitting around their claws or hands or whatever they had.

With a desperate yank, she dragged Quinn backward, through the threshold.

They had no right to make it.

But they did.

The restroom swallowed them whole, the door slamming shut behind them with a force that rattled the frame.

Stephanie didn't stop. She hauled Quinn into the nearest stall and shoved the door shut, slamming the flimsy metal latch into place with shaking hands. It was nothing—thin steel, a cheap lock—but it was all they had.

She pressed her back against the cold wall at the rear of the stall. Quinn bent forward at the front, bracing herself with shaking hands on her knees, breaths coming in ragged, rapid gasps.

The bathroom was silent.

Too silent.

A silence that rang in Stephanie's skull after the cacophony outside. She held her breath and listened.

Nothing.

But she didn't trust that quiet for a second.

Not now. Not here. Not after what they'd just seen.

No sound came from beyond the stall door.

The silence felt wrong—too clean, too still—given the hell they'd escaped only seconds before. The suffocating heat was gone. The reek of sulfur and rot had evaporated. Even the paralyzing pressure that had wrapped around Stephanie's lungs like barbed wire had loosened its grip.

In the quiet, their breathing slowly steadied. Stephanie felt her shoulders drop, the tension bleeding out of her muscles. Quinn wiped at her eyes, chest rising and falling in small, trembling breaths.

They were alive. Unharmed. Back in a restroom that looked exactly as it had before.

A soft, weary laugh escaped Stephanie as relief washed over her—so fragile it felt like it might crack if she breathed too hard. Quinn gave her a matching, shaky smile.

Minutes passed. Still no sound. Still no threat. For the first time since they'd arrived at the bar, the world was quiet.

Stephanie reached out, wanting nothing more than to pull Quinn into a hug and anchor both of them to something that felt human.

Quinn took a small step forward—

—and froze.

Her hands snapped up to grip Stephanie's forearms with a panic so sharp it cut through the air.

Stephanie followed her gaze downward.

Two hands—if they could be called hands—wrapped around Quinn's ankles. Skin sloughed off in black, wet ribbons. Fingers ended in swollen, purpled nails. The stench of rot rose from them in a choking wave.

Stephanie's scream tangled with Quinn's as Quinn's feet were yanked violently out from under her. She pitched forward, crashing into Stephanie's arms. Their hands locked together, knuckles whitening, muscles straining.

"Please—Stephanie—don't let me go!" Quinn sobbed, brown eyes wide, drowning in terror.

"I've got you! I've got you!" Stephanie choked out, bracing her leg behind her, pressing her shoulder into the tiled wall for leverage. "Hold on, Quinn—just hold on—"

Quinn was ripped backward.

Her body slammed to the floor hard enough to knock the breath from her lungs, her scream shattering into raw, ragged pieces. Stephanie's grip slipped—slick with sweat, trembling with panic—and then Quinn was wrenched beneath the stall door.

Stephanie lurched forward, losing her balance. Her head struck the metal with a hollow, cracking thud. Black spots burst behind her eyes. She didn't even register her own scream at first.

Her fingers fumbled at the latch. It rattled wildly beneath her shaking hands.

Quinn's screams ripped through the bathroom—

—until they didn't.

Until they cut off mid-cry.

Silence slammed into the room like a physical force.

Stephanie flung the stall door open so hard it bounced off the divider. She stumbled out, nearly falling. "Quinn!" she screamed, voice shredded from fear.

She kicked open the next stall.

Empty.

Cold.

Still.

Gone.

Her sob broke through the quiet, raw and hopeless, echoing off the tile walls.

Chapter Nine

Chris watched Karen drift out from behind the bar, heading toward the stranger who had chosen a table near the middle of the room. His attention flickered—half on her, half on the mess sitting at his feet.

John had decided that the safest place for him tonight was the floor. Not a chair, not a barstool—just planted right there on the grimy boards, legs sprawled out, head wobbling as he tried to stay upright. Getting him to stand was like convincing a toddler to walk during a tantrum. Chris tugged, braced, tugged again. Nothing.

What bothered Chris almost as much as John's stubbornness was Karen's indifference to the fact that a drunk minor was sitting on her floor like a discarded rag doll. No raised eyebrow. No sigh. Not even a "get him up." She passed them with the same empty expression she might give a stain on the counter.

She stopped beside the newcomer and flipped open her notepad, bored down to the bone.

"What can I get for you, sir? Kitchen's closed. Drinks only."

"Just call me Aaron," he said, distracted, like her presence barely registered. "A soda's fine."

Karen eyed him a moment—measuring trouble the way bartenders can—then turned to walk back to the bar. "All we have is cola," she tossed over her shoulder.

Chris let the stranger fade from his mind. He had bigger issues. He sank into a chair beside John, who still refused to lift his rear off the floor, and tried to get more out of him about the bizarre loop he described earlier—leaving the bar only to end up right back here.

Everything John had said matched what Chris, Babs, Stephanie, and Quinn had experienced on the road. And yet John was too fried—emotionally and mentally—to help him piece together any way out of this place.

Chris leaned back, the chair creaking under him, and let out a low sound of disgust. Partly at the nightmare they were in. Mostly at John—slumped, glassy-eyed, reeking of tequila.

Movement flickered in his periphery. A woman sidled up.

The same woman who'd approached him earlier—right before John rammed a broken bottle into Tank's throat.

Pinky.

She nudged his chair out from the table with her foot and slid onto his lap without waiting for permission.

"Mind if I join you?" she asked, already settled comfortably, as if she'd always belonged there.

Chris didn't get a vote. Her weight pinned him to the seat. Her perfume drowned out any remaining thoughts of John, or the stranger, or the growing stretch of time Stephanie and Quinn had been gone. Everything else blurred to static.

Across the room, Tank and Romeo glared at him—lips curling, eyes tracking every inch of Pinky's body pressed against his. Chris didn't notice. Pinky occupied his entire field of view.

Henry, meanwhile, was trapped in his own uneasy world—a thousand-yard stare toward nothing. Babs sat near him, shifting anxiously on her stool. She kept glancing toward the hallway leading to the restrooms, measuring the length of time her friends had been gone, calculating whether she could check on them alone.

She didn't want to walk past the pool tables where the bikers gathered—and she definitely didn't want to do it wearing her cheer outfit, bare legs exposed under the short skirt. Tank and Romeo hadn't stopped staring at her since the moment they walked in. She could feel their eyes crawling over her.

She considered asking Henry to walk with her, but he was too distracted to register anything outside his head.

So she stayed put. For now.

She glanced again at Tank and Romeo. Both men were seated to her right, their gazes sticky and unbroken. The skirt she'd once thought was cute now felt like bait. She wished she'd worn pants—anything with fabric that didn't leave her feeling skinned open.

She resolved to scoot over to Henry's other side—to put an extra human barrier between her and the bikers.

But before she could move, Henry abruptly stood and walked toward the restrooms. Alone.

Perfect timing, she thought bitterly.

Now she was exposed on both sides.

She scanned the bar for Chris and John, hoping one of them might be sober—or aware—enough to act as a buffer. Chris was preoccupied with Pinky. John was barely conscious.

Tank shifted first, sliding off his stool and stepping toward her. Romeo mirrored him, cutting off her escape from the other direction.

Babs pressed back until her spine hit the bar. Her breath hitched as both men moved in, close enough that their heat radiated through her clothes.

Fear rolled off her in waves—so strong she could feel it vibrating in her fingertips.

And the men drank it in like animals scenting blood.

Tank leaned closer, the sour mix of whiskey and cigarettes heavy on his breath.

Romeo's chest brushed her arm, blocking out her light, her space, her air.

The room felt like it was shrinking around her.

Like the bar itself was swallowing her up.

And no one—not Chris, not Henry, not even John—noticed.

Babs turned toward Romeo—and ran straight into his fractured, toothy grin. His breath hit her first. Sour. Wet. Fetid. Not alcohol. Not cigarettes. Something deeper, something rotting. Tank's breath was the same—the stink of decaying flesh rolling off both men in hot waves.

They were too close. Far too close. Close enough that Babs could see every pore, every crease, every wrongness in their faces—and the need to escape rose in her chest like a trapped scream.

Tank leaned in and inhaled deeply against her hair, a long, slow sniff.

Babs jerked back, bile climbing her throat. The smell—God, the smell—was enough to make her vomit. She slapped a hand over her nose and mouth, barely stopping herself from retching.

Up close, Tank's face was wrong in ways her mind couldn't process quickly enough. His skin looked... stretched. Plasticky. As if it didn't quite belong to him. Beneath it—she was sure this wasn't her imagination—shapes wriggled. Something squirmed under the surface, shifting from cheekbone to jaw in a slow, serpentine ripple.

She tore her eyes away—and instantly regretted turning to Romeo.

At first glance he looked more normal. But only at first.

The longer she looked, the more his skin resembled a poorly fitted mask—loose in places, too tight in others. A thin gap yawned beside his eyes, a dark seam that shouldn't exist. And those eyes—glazed, cloudy, unfocused—looked like the lifeless stare of a wax figure, not a living man.

Her stomach lurched again.

She didn't get to look any longer.

A hand slid through the strands of hair escaping the bun on her head, twining itself there.

Tank.

She snapped her head away—but he moved faster. His hand clamped around her chin, fingers digging in like iron hooks. Babs' hands flew up to yank his wrist off her face—

And her fingers sank into something soft.

Not skin. Not muscle. Something yielding, like cold putty. Something slick.

She gasped.

Tears spilled down her cheeks as Tank's grip tightened, forcing her head still. Her fingers slipped uselessly along his wrist—too slimy to grasp. Terror pinned her in place, suffocating, overwhelming, indescribable.

Her eyes darted toward Chris. She let out a broken whimper.

But Chris didn't even glance her way.

Pinky sat on his lap, all perfume and heavy limbs and alcohol-soaked heat, her presence wrapped around him like a spell. He didn't see Babs pinned against the bar. Didn't see Tank's hand on her chin. Didn't see Romeo crowding her from the other side.

John was nowhere in sight.

Henry had vanished.

Stephanie and Quinn still hadn't returned.

Babs was alone.

Her scream ripped out of her when Romeo's hand slid up the bare skin of her leg. She kicked wildly, trying to dislodge him—but he snarled, grabbed her skirt, and tore it straight off her hips. The sharp crack of his slap was louder than the music, louder than the pool balls, louder than anything.

The welt rose on her cheek instantly.

And that—finally—cut through Chris's haze.

He snapped his head toward the bar in time to see Romeo's hand snap back from slapping her. Rage surged hot in his chest. He shoved his hands against Pinky's sides, trying to force her off his lap—

A flash of metal froze him cold.

Pinky held a switchblade inches from his eye.

"Don't even think about moving, pretty boy," she purred. The wicked gleam in her eyes told him she meant every word. "Let my friends play with the little girl... while I keep playing with you."

Her free hand slid behind his neck, fingers spidering up his nape. She yanked him forward, burying his face in her chest, blocking his vision entirely. The blade kissed the skin of his throat, cold and unyielding.

"You stay right here," she whispered. "Be good for me."

Chris tried to turn his head—but she sealed her mouth to his. The kiss was hard, invasive, her lips crushing his, teeth scraping, tongue forcing hers way past his. Her breath was thick with whiskey and rot.

When she finally pulled back, it was only to reposition herself—lifting slightly, shifting her hips, sliding from a sideways perch into a full straddle, facing him directly, thighs locking around him like a trap.

He couldn't see Babs at all now.

He couldn't see anything except her.

And behind him—unseen—Babs trembled in nothing but her bloomers, pinned between two monsters wearing the faces of men.

Chris's instincts surged like a lightning strike—every muscle ready to stand, shove Pinky to the floor, and sprint to Babs before those two monsters could lay another hand on her. He was a breath away from doing it.

But the blade decided otherwise.

When Pinky shifted her weight on his lap, she'd subtly moved the knife. The cold, thin edge that had threatened his eye now rested against the tender skin of his throat. Chris felt the metal kiss his flesh—just enough pressure to promise that a twitch, a cough, even a sharp inhale would split him open from ear to ear.

If he moved, he died.

If he died, Babs was done for.

The helplessness carved through him deeper than the blade ever could. He could see her fear—her shoulders trembling, her breath hitching, her body rigid between Tank and Romeo. Every second he sat there felt like a betrayal. He had the strength. He had the will. He could end them both if that knife weren't at his throat.

His jaw clenched. He tasted blood from biting down too hard.

Babs, for her part, knew he saw her. Their eyes had met—her pleading, his burning with trapped fury. She understood why he couldn't move. She didn't blame him. She didn't have time to.

Her mind scrambled for someone, anyone, who could help.

Henry—gone.

John—lost in his own hell.

Stephanie and Quinn—still in the restroom.

Maybe they would hear her if she screamed—although three terrified girls against two hulking men was hardly a fair fight. But terror does strange things to logic, and survival doesn't require fairness—just opportunity.

She inhaled, ready to scream—

—but the wind never made it out.

Romeo's fist slammed into her stomach with brutal force.

"We cain't have ya screamin' no more," he growled, voice thick with malice.

The punch folded her in half. Her vision blurred. Her knees buckled. Tank jerked her head upright again, forcing her to face forward while she gasped for breath, tears streaking down her cheeks as her diaphragm spasmed uselessly. She could barely stand, barely think, barely exist past the agony.

She felt herself slipping—mind, strength, hope.

And then help came.

It arrived as a blur of motion, a dark streak in the corner of her eye—too fast to identify, but when it connected with Tank's jaw, crimson sprayed across the bar in an arc.

Tank dropped like someone had cut his strings.

Before she could process it, the object blurred back the other direction—connecting with Romeo's skull with a wet, sickening crack. He collapsed beside Tank in a twitching heap.

When the blur resolved into a form, Babs saw him.

John.

He stood before her, a baseball bat in hand, breath heaving, eyes blazing. Relief hit her so forcefully she nearly collapsed into him.

Behind them, Chris seized his chance.

While Pinky reacted to the sudden violence, her grip on the blade loosened just slightly. Chris twisted her wrist with practiced force. She shrieked, the knife clattering against the floorboards as her fingers spasmed open.

Chris shoved her—hard.

She toppled to the ground with a smack that promised bruises. Maybe worse. He didn't give her a second thought. He was on his feet, free of her weight, free of her trap, in the same instant.

Babs clung to John's side, trembling, her cheek swollen from Romeo's slap, her bare legs streaked with grime now that her skirt hung in tatters. Apart from the bruises rising along her ribs and jaw, she would live. And John—despite how drunk he'd been—had regained every ounce of clarity he needed to save her.

Chris took stock of the scene.

Tank lay motionless.

Romeo... moved, but barely.

Both had taken blows that should have put them down for good.

John gripped the baseball bat in his right hand, the heft of the wood suddenly comforting. The anger that had simmered in him since arriving here now aligned with something sharper—resolve.

He stepped toward John to clap him on the back, to tell him "good job, man," to reclaim some control of this nightmare—

—but he froze.

Something was wrong.

Very wrong.

Romeo rose.

Slowly. Jerkingly. His neck twisted at an unnatural angle before snapping back into place with a wet pop. Blood soaked half his face, and the side of his skull—where the bat had made direct contact—was caved in, mangled beyond anything humanly survivable.

He smiled anyway.

A ghastly, shredded thing.

"Well now... that weren't very kind at all," he slurred, stepping forward with grotesque determination.

John positioned himself between Romeo and Babs, shifting her behind him. He stepped forward, giving himself room to swing. Hands tightening around the bat, he drew back, ready to knock that monstrous grin off Romeo's face—

A tug on his right side sent his swing off-balance.

John turned—

Tank was standing.

Right beside him.

Tank's ruined hand closed around the end of the bat, halting John's swing with impossible ease. Up close, Tank's head looked even worse than Romeo's—softened, caved in, pulped like an overripe melon. It was a miracle his skull still held together. One eye dangled from the socket, swaying slightly, connected only by a thin thread of optic nerve.

He should have been blind. He should have been dead.

But Tank turned that dangling eye toward John with uncanny accuracy.

Before John could recover from the shock, Tank jerked the bat with a vicious twist—quick, precise, mechanical.

John's scream tore through the bar as he dropped to his knees, clutching his right wrist. His hand hung at an unnatural angle, shredded and limp, attached only by flaps of torn skin.

Babs dropped beside him, bracing him by the shoulders as he swayed, dizzy with pain.

Then everything dimmed.

A shadow fell over them.

Babs looked up—slowly, because every instinct begged her not to—and found Tank looming above them. He now held the bat in both hands, lifting it high, preparing to bring it down. The angle, the force behind his stance—one blow would kill them both.

The moment froze, suspended on the edge of terror.

And then—

A new sound cut through the paralysis.

A metallic click.

Babs turned her head in time to see the stranger from earlier—Aaron—draw a revolver from inside his coat with frightening calm.

He didn't hesitate.

He didn't shout a warning.

He simply aimed.

And fired.

The muzzle flash burst like white lightning, followed by a thunderous crack that shook the walls. The impact tore Tank's head apart in a spray of shadow and smoke. His body staggered forward, slammed into the bar, and collapsed—

Then burst into green flame.

The fire burned unnaturally bright, neon and acidic, filling the air with the bitter stench of brimstone and wyrmwood. The body crumbled into ash in seconds, the flames vanishing in a puff of oily black smoke.

Aaron didn't even watch it finish burning.

He turned sharply toward Babs.

"Get him up and get out of here!"

Then, snapping his gaze to Chris:

"Help her!"

Chris jolted into motion.

But he froze again mid-stride.

Because behind Aaron—Romeo was rising.

Head hanging backward, neck split nearly to the spine, body lifting as if pulled by invisible strings.

Without turning fully around, Aaron fired again.

The shot punched through Romeo's chest with explosive force. The biker flew backward several feet before erupting in the same green fire. His severed head rolled to a stop, catching flame an instant later.

Chris's mind barely processed the sequence. It felt unreal—disjointed—like he was watching frames of film instead of reality. But shock didn't stop his body. He ran to Babs, grabbing John under the good arm while Babs supported his other side.

Across the bar, chaos erupted.

The remaining bikers surged toward Aaron with roars of fury. Pinky and Karen bolted for the back of the bar, scrambling over stools in their panic. The floor vibrated under the thunder of boots, the crack of gunfire, the hiss of burning bodies.

Chris, Babs, and John moved.

They ran.

They didn't stop.

With Aaron close behind them, they sprinted toward the bar's front door as the nightmare finally broke loose behind them.

Part Three
Chapter Ten

Babs was falling behind.

Chris set a brutal pace, half-dragging, half-carrying John between them, and her shorter legs just couldn't keep up. John leaned most of his weight on Chris, barely using Babs at all, but she refused to let go. She didn't want to look at his hand—God, she didn't want to—but every few steps her eyes dropped anyway.

His wrist was swollen to the size of a softball and still ballooning. Blood seeped through torn skin, but most of it was pooling under the surface, distorting the flesh. Only a thin band of tissue and ragged skin seemed to be keeping the hand attached at all.

They needed a tourniquet. Soon. Or John was going to bleed out or pass out—or both.

Aaron followed a few steps behind, revolver still in hand. Babs kept glancing back to make sure he was there. It was a strange comfort and a new kind of fear at the same time. He was the only one who seemed to know what he was doing—and he was the one with the gun.

When they burst out of Ruby's Place, the night air hit her like something remembered from another life. Too much had happened since they'd first walked in. No amount of gory TV or movie violence could have prepared her for what she'd just lived through.

She would've traded anything to wake up in her own bed and chalk this up to a nightmare. But waking up didn't seem to be on the menu.

Aaron jerked his chin toward the dark hulk of the abandoned garage instead of toward the lot where Chris's car sat.

"This way," he said.

That was all. No explanation. No time to argue.

Babs had assumed they'd pile into the car and bolt, but she was beyond thinking strategy now. John was bleeding. That was as far as her planning went.

They reached the front of the garage and scanned for a way in. Aaron motioned them around back.

"You two first," he said, staying behind them as rear guard, gun slightly lowered but still ready.

At the rear door, Babs gently eased John more fully onto Chris and tried the handle. It didn't budge. She jiggled it once more in disbelief.

"It's locked," she said, more to herself than anyone else.

She stared at the door, brain stuck on the idea that someone had bothered to secure this rotting building. To keep people out so they wouldn't get hurt? Or to keep something inside?

She opened her mouth to suggest they look for a window when Aaron stepped up beside her. He shifted her out of the way with one hand—firm, not brutal, but with a kind of casual force that brooked no argument.

Then he kicked the door.

The wood gave with a splintering crack, swinging inward and sagging on ruined hinges. Aaron slipped in first, revolver leading the way, barrel tracking across every corner of the gloom. He moved with practiced efficiency, his gun defining a quick, invisible sweep of danger zones.

"Clear enough," he said finally, with a short nod. "Bring him in."

Babs and Chris guided John inside. Aaron hauled the door back up and shoved it roughly into the frame to block most of the outside light.

Inside, it was dim and stale. The only illumination seeped in through the gaps around the boarded windows, colored faintly by the neon glare bleeding over from Ruby's Place. A harsh, flickering wash of pinks and greens painted everything in thin, uneven layers.

Someone had nailed boards not only over the outside of the windows but along the inside too. Shards of filthy glass still clung to some of the frames. Dust and grime coated the floor, walls, even the ceiling—like the whole room had been abandoned mid-breath and left to molder.

Near them, an overturned chair lay on its side. Babs grabbed it, set it upright, and—with Chris's help—eased John down into it.

Her next thought was simple and sharp: stop the bleeding.

She scanned the room for anything she could use as a tourniquet, barely listening at first when Chris started talking to John. But his voice still carried in the hollow space.

"John, what the hell have you gotten us into?" Chris demanded, crouching in front of him. "This is some very weird shit. I know I've said that already, but I still don't have an answer."

John cradled his arm against his chest, fingers pressed above the wreck of his wrist. He rocked slowly, not because it helped the pain, but because it gave his body something to do besides collapse.

His face twisted in a mix of anger and misery.

"This is that damn bar you told me about," he rasped. "The one where we could get alcohol without needing ID."

There was an accusation buried in John's words—one Chris wasn't about to let slide.

Chris exhaled sharply, chest rising and falling as he snapped, "You wanna pin this shit on me? You're the one who asked where somebody could get beer without needing ID. I just told you what I knew. I never suggested we all come out to this fucking place. That was your call."

He pushed to his feet, pacing a few steps toward one of the grime-coated windows. The neon glow bleeding through didn't help anything feel real or sane.

"Look," he said, turning back to John, "I didn't want to come here. But you said you wanted everyone together again. It felt like... I don't know. Like maybe I owed you guys that much. I know I walked out of everyone's lives, but hanging out without all the pressure and bullshit sounded like something I should at least show up for."

He gestured wide, arms sweeping at the dust-choked garage, the boarded windows, the memory of the carnage they'd escaped.

"I told you about this place, sure—but I never heard anything about this."

John lifted his head. His face was pale, drawn tight with pain. "I don't know what's going on either, Chris. I swear I don't. Henry and I got here, and everything went sideways right after. It feels like... like I've been here for weeks already." His voice dropped to a hoarse whisper. "I keep going through the same thing over and over. Like it resets. Nothing stopped until you and the girls showed up."

Chris crouched down beside him. John looked almost hollow, like whatever he'd lived through had scraped his nerves raw.

"John, talk to me," Chris said quietly. "How the hell could you be here a week when the game only ended a few hours ago?"

John grabbed a fistful of Chris's shirt with his good hand, yanking him closer. Panic glinted in his eyes. "This place is a nightmare, Chris. Check the date on your phone." His voice cracked. "I'm telling you—we've been trapped here a week."

Chris pried John's fingers off and rocked back on his heels. He pulled out his phone and held it up.

"It's dead, man. Been dead for an hour."

John's roar of frustration echoed through the garage. Babs jumped where she was rummaging for supplies, but she didn't interfere.

"Fine," John growled. "Get mine. Check the date. I'm not crazy."

Chris reached into John's pocket, fished out the phone, and turned it on—nothing. No light. No charge.

John's breath hitched. "Well? I'm right, huh?"

Chris showed him the blank screen. "It's dead too. Just like everybody's."

"That's not right." John shook his head, wincing from the motion. "It never died. Not once. I kept checking it every day. Every fucking day."

The pain overwhelmed him suddenly. He curled protectively around his ruined wrist, shoulders shaking as a low sob escaped him.

"Hey." Chris stood and gripped John's shoulders. "Stay with me. Just tell me what happened."

John lifted his head, desperation written clear across his face. "I've killed Tank over and over again," he whispered. "I've done it a hundred different ways and it keeps resetting. None of it stuck. Nothing changed until you all showed up."

Chris noticed the repetition but didn't interrupt.

John blinked, confusion wrinkling his brow. "Sometimes I couldn't remember it clearly. Like it'd blur. I'd get flashes that felt like déjà vu. Then it'd start all over again."

Anger surged in him suddenly—wild, hot, and misdirected. "Are you sure you're not drunk?" Chris asked cautiously.

John shoved him away with his good hand. "You don't believe me?"

Chris shook his head slowly. "I'm not saying that. I just... I don't know what to believe anymore. You've been drinking all night. I don't know how much you had before we got here. I think you believe what you're saying. But this—" He gestured helplessly. "This isn't real life."

John stared at him, slack-jawed. Then his expression curdled. "Fuck you, Chris. I'm not drunk. And I'm not crazy. This place is fucked up."

He turned away, hunching around his mangled wrist.

The dim lighting made it impossible for Babs to read Aaron's face, so she didn't try. Instead, she forced a small, tired smile.

"I'm fine. And... yeah. I found what I needed," she murmured, holding up a rag and a small length of pipe pressed against her chest. Her voice dropped even further. "I should go help John."

She slipped around the corner. Aaron followed in silence, footsteps soft and controlled.

Both boys turned toward her when she dropped to a crouch beside John's right side.

"I found some stuff for a tourniquet," Babs said, breath unsteady. "But nothing to actually wrap the wrist."

John shifted his gaze to Chris.

"Help me get out of my jacket. Then my shirt—we can use that."

Babs raised a hand.

"That's going to hurt, John. A lot. And you'll freeze faster than the rest of us if you lose more layers. Your body can't handle more shock."

John hesitated. For the first time, resolve wavered behind his pain-tightened features.

"If you've got scissors or a knife, we can cut the sleeve off."

Babs' lips tightened. She shook her head and looked down her body.

Cheerleader outfit. Minus the discarded ruined skirt. Leaving only bloomers—cheer short—and a letterman jacket.

"Why would I have either of those?"

Chris checked his pockets hoping he'd slipped his pocket knife somewhere, then gave the same answer—nothing.

"Figures," John muttered. The idea of cutting the shirt instead of shifting his mangled hand had been a brief hope, and now it was gone. "Fine. Help me with the jacket."

Chris moved reluctantly, fully aware of what this would cost John. The process was slow, agonizing, and ugly—John gritted his teeth through every second of it. When the jacket finally came off, Chris didn't bother with John's shirt. Instead, he tore off the bottom portion of his own and handed it to Babs.

"That'll work," she said softly.

She wound the fabric around what was left of John's wrist, cinched the pipe as a windlass, and then used the rag to fashion a makeshift sling across his chest. It wasn't pretty, but it elevated the arm and slowed the bleeding.

John didn't bother hiding the pain. There was no point—not from Babs, not from Chris, not from anyone. Pride didn't matter anymore. Surviving did.

When she finished, Aaron stepped out of the shadows again. He inspected her work with a single, approving nod, then moved to the boarded window to resume scanning the outside.

Babs followed his movement briefly, curious what Chris thought of the stranger's looming presence. Chris, exhausted and stretched thin, didn't seem to care who Aaron was—only that he wasn't attacking them.

Chris helped John to his feet and eased him against the wall, lowering him to sit with his back supported.

"Stay here. If you doze off, you won't fall," Chris said.

John nodded and closed his eyes, trying to breathe through the pain.

"Chris," Babs whispered.

He joined her a few steps away.

"What's up?"

"We need to get him to a hospital soon." Her eyes flicked to John. "If we wait too long, he's going to bleed out. And we can't leave that tourniquet on forever."

Chris followed her gaze, then shook his head.

"Even if we get him to a hospital, they can't reattach that hand."

"That's not the point," Babs hissed. "I don't want him to die. Losing the hand is one thing. Losing him is another."

Chris scrubbed a hand over his face. "I know. I was thinking the same thing. But we're not leaving anyone behind. We have to find Stephanie, Quinn, and Henry first."

"We don't even know if they're still in the bar," Babs whispered. "How the hell are we supposed to find them?"

Chris pulled out his phone again, flicking at the dead screen in frustration.

"We could call Stephanie—if her phone wasn't dead too."

Babs's eyes blinked rapidly. Something nagged at the edge of her mind, but before she could grasp it—

"Your friends are still in the bar."

Aaron hadn't turned. His attention remained fixed between the slats in the boarded window. But his voice echoed across the room like a verdict.

Chris straightened.

He'd been waiting for this—answers, or at least something resembling them.

"Who are you?" Chris demanded.

Aaron finally turned his head just enough to look at him. His expression held the same disdain one might reserve for an insect on a windshield.

"Aaron."

Chris's jaw tightened.

"That's not what I asked. What do you know about what's happening here?"

Aaron paused, considering.

He looked like a man weighing the value of each possible word before allowing it to leave his mouth.

"Well," he said at last, "I know it doesn't matter what I tell you right now."

He shifted his stance, stepping away from the wall, subtly adjusting his angle toward Chris and Babs.

Neither of them noticed the significance of that shift.

"It does matter," Chris insisted. "You clearly know something you're not telling us. We're caught up in this too—and one of my friends is seriously hurt."

He gestured toward John, still slumped against the wall.

Aaron didn't flinch. "Your other friends are still inside that building." He pointed toward the bar entrance. "That's what matters.

Getting them out needs to be the priority. Once you're all together, then you leave."

Chris turned to Babs, silently asking her to back him up, but she said nothing. Still shaken, still processing, she wasn't ready to challenge the only competent fighter in the room.

Frustration surged through Chris, but he forced himself to focus.

"Fine," he said sharply. "We do need them. I'll go get them, and when I get back, we're all getting out of here. And then—" his gaze hardened "—I'm getting answers from you."

Aaron raised one hand, palm toward Chris, telling him to wait. He glanced through the boarded window again.

"What?" Chris demanded. "Someone out there?"

"No," Aaron replied—calm, infuriatingly calm. "Not yet. They're reorganizing. I don't know if they'll come after us first or hunt your friends. That's why we need them now."

"Okay," Chris repeated, exasperated. "I'll go—"

Aaron stepped directly into his path, shoulders squared.

"No."

The word hit like a physical stop.

"You stay here with her. And him."

He pointed to Babs, then John.

Before Chris could argue, Aaron moved to the exit, cracked the door just enough to slip through, then paused to look back at Babs—not Chris.

"If I'm not back in twenty minutes," he said, voice low and carved with finality, "take your injured friend and go."

He stepped out. The door clicked shut behind him.

Babs darted to the boarded window, just in time to catch a glimpse of Aaron striding across the lot toward the bar, his revolver glinting under the neon glow. In seconds, he vanished into the darkness.

Inside, she heard a shift of movement.

Chris was heading for the door on the opposite side—the one leading deeper into the abandoned garage.

"Where are you going?" she hissed.

John had finally fallen asleep—restless, sweating, but asleep. The last thing she wanted was to wake him.

"I'm checking the rest of this building," Chris said. "You watch him. And keep an eye out for that stranger. I want to leave the second the others get back."

Babs hesitated. Panic clawed at her chest.

"I—Chris, what about John? I can't take care of him alone. What if something happens? I'm too small."

Chris gave a short laugh—too sharp, too tired.

"Something has already happened, Babs. Look at his hand." He gestured toward John's swollen, mangled wrist. "Look at everything. We left this place and ended up right back here—twice."

He stepped toward her.

Babs instinctively stepped back.

He stopped, incredulous.

"*Really?*"

He shook his head and gestured toward the boarded windows.

"Did you see what happened when that guy shot Tank and Romeo?"

Babs nodded, trembling.

"They shouldn't have moved after John hit them," Chris said. "But they did. He shot them—and they burst into green flames. Green flames, Babs. What else do you think can happen?"

His words struck harder than he intended.

Her face crumpled. Tears slid down her cheeks before she could stop them.

Chris exhaled sharply.

"I'm sorry," he said quickly. "I didn't mean to make you feel stupid."

Sniffling, voice small, Babs whispered, "I'm scared. I don't know what to do. And I don't want you to leave me."

Chris stepped closer again—slowly this time.

She didn't retreat.

He opened his arms, giving her the choice.

After a brief hesitation, she stepped into him, burying her face against his chest. He wrapped his arms around her and gently patted the back of her head.

He was warm. A little too warm. She chalked it up to her state of dress or him being feverish himself and remained where she was.

"Look, I get it. I'm scared too," he said softly. "Anybody would be. I don't know one person who'd be calm right now."

He leaned back just enough to meet her eyes, offering her a steadying smile.

"I don't trust that stranger," he admitted. "And we don't have anything to defend ourselves with. I need to look around—see if there's something we can use. A tool, a pipe, anything. It's the only way I'll feel comfortable when he gets back."

Despite herself, Babs nodded.

His logic made sense. They had nothing. Aaron had a gun. And everything inside the bar was impossible.

"Okay," she whispered.

"I won't be long."

He kissed her lightly on the forehead—unexpectedly tender—then released her and stepped toward the doorway.

Babs still hated the idea of Chris leaving her. The garage felt too big, too dark, and too quiet with John unconscious and bleeding beside her. But Chris had understood her fear—really understood it—and had tried, for once, to reassure her. And he was right: they needed a weapon. They didn't know if the stranger would return before someone from the bar followed their trail.

She didn't want to be alone, and she didn't want to be unarmed.

Between the two evils, the need for survival won out.

So she let him go, hoping that the faster he left, the faster he would come back. If she'd been thinking straight, she realized, she should have searched for something herself while gathering things for John.

Chris slipped through the doorway and moved cautiously across the automotive bay. The dim overhead lights cast long, uneven shadows, and he hugged the perimeter, avoiding the dark center of the room where the pit openings might be. He could barely make them out—just long black rectangles in the concrete. One wrong step in the dark, and he could vanish into one.

The garage was wide enough to service four cars at once, so crossing it took longer than he expected. On the far side, he spotted two small offices, the gaping doorway of a rank-smelling restroom, and a narrow staircase. The stairs likely led either down to storage or into the maintenance pits under the floor.

Chris stepped toward them—and froze.

A sharp scrape echoed through the stillness.

A shoe dragging on concrete.

He reacted instantly, ducking into the nearest office. His breath hitched—just as a figure appeared at the far side of the room.

Pinky.

Her eyes glowed red like coals catching a spark.

Before Chris could retreat or shout, she lunged.

The violent collision slammed him backward, the impact echoing through the garage like a gunshot.

The sound jolted Babs upright.

Her heart slammed in her chest. That wasn't a stumble. That wasn't a tool dropped on the floor. That was Chris. And it was far too loud.

There was no way Chris would be that careless. Not now. Not after everything.

A noise that loud could carry outside—straight to the bar. Straight to the people they were hiding from.

Babs waited—tense, breath held, praying for another sound. A groan. A shout. Footsteps. Anything.

But nothing came.

The silence pressed in on her, thick and suffocating.

Finally, she swallowed her fear and stepped away from John's side.

She didn't want to go.

She didn't have a choice.

And within moments, she found the truth—

and with it, even more questions.

Chapter Eleven

Aaron moved with deliberate caution as he cut across the open space between the abandoned garage and the bar. His eyes swept the darkness, tracking every shift of shadow, every possible angle of approach. The bikers—or rather, what wore their bodies—could be lying in wait. He couldn't afford to return to the kids injured... or not at all.

They complicated everything.

His mission had been simple: clear the infestation, cleanse the ground, move on. But the moment he saw the kids, everything shifted. Innocents always changed the calculus.

He exhaled slowly, letting the tension bleed off his shoulders. Complications or not, the priority was clear now:

Keep the kids alive.

Then clean house.

Two demons down.

Five more, by his last estimation.

Probably the bartender, maybe some of the regulars near the pool tables. Nothing he couldn't handle—so long as they didn't swarm.

He reached the bar's entrance without incident. A quick scan confirmed the stillness outside. He pushed the door open lightly and stepped into the dim, stagnant air.

The smell hit immediately.

Ordinarily, identifying Infernals was easy. Lesser demons always carried the same signature rot—sour, wet death. To most people it was faint, maybe dismissible. But to him, it was a beacon.

Here, the scent was everywhere. Saturated. Baked into the walls.

And layered over it, the harsh sting of brimstone and wyrmwood from the two he'd already destroyed—enough to drown out lesser trails completely.

Aaron clicked his tongue in irritation.

This was going to be annoying.

The bar appeared empty.

No shambling figures.

No half-worn faces or drifting eyes.

No movement at all.

Good.

Maybe his luck would hold long enough to get the rest of the kids out.

He pictured the missing three—two girls who had gone toward the restrooms, and the boy who'd wandered off. He remembered seeing the girls last, which narrowed the search.

He crossed the room quickly and paused at the narrow hallway. The men's restroom door was closed. He passed it without stopping and placed his hand on the women's door, pushing it open with small, controlled pressure.

No movement.

He stepped inside.

To the left: sinks.

To the right: two stalls.

He nudged the first door open with his boot. Empty.

The second stall was shut tight.

He leaned down just enough to check beneath the door—not seeing legs didn't mean anything. He didn't like kneeling; that put him at a disadvantage. Scaling the adjacent toilet would be even worse.

Direct, then.

"Hey," he called lightly. "Anybody in there?"

Silence.

He tried again, louder this time. "Your friends sent me to get you."

Still nothing.

Aaron sighed, clearing his throat.

"All right. I'm kicking this in. Stall door opens inward. If you're behind it, it's gonna hurt. I'm counting to three."

He backed up, giving himself room.

"One. Two—"

"Hold on!"

A young woman's panicked voice.

The latch clicked.

The stall door eased open, and Stephanie stepped out, wide-eyed and cautious. Aaron's gaze swept her quickly—checking limbs, posture, breathing. No visible injuries. No demonic distortion.

She stared at him. "Who are you?"

Aaron had already lowered the revolver the moment she appeared. No point in spooking her more than she already was.

"Someone who's here to help," he said.

And it landed exactly as it should: calm, steady, competent—as if he'd said this a hundred times before.

"My name's Aaron," he said. "I came to get you and take you back to Chris, Babs, and John."

He didn't waste time. He gently took Stephanie by the arm and moved her aside so he could check the stall behind her—even though he already knew no one else was inside.

"Are you alone?" he asked.

Stephanie stared at him blankly. She glanced back into the stall, then back at him. Her jaw worked, trying to form words, but none came. Aaron recognized the look instantly.

Shock.

He reholstered the revolver and leaned in just enough to center her attention.

"Eyes on me," he murmured.

Stephanie's gaze flicked up to his—and Aaron clapped his hands once, sharply. The sound cracked through the fog clouding her mind. She flinched, blinking fast, breath catching.

"Hey, kid. You with me?" he asked, softer now.

She shook her head once, clearing it. "Yeah. I'm good," she said—more to convince herself than him.

"Okay. Are you alone? Where's the other girl?"

Stephanie's eyes drifted toward the door. When she spoke, her voice trembled.

"We left the restroom... but when we stepped out, it wasn't the bar. Everything was gone. It was like a wasteland. Those things were everywhere. Something grabbed her legs and pulled her under the stall door. I couldn't hold on. I came out to look for her and she wasn't here. Then I heard two gunshots, and I... I hid."

Aaron absorbed the words quickly. The gunshots had been his, so he dismissed that part—but everything else mattered.

Especially the door.

He studied it, leaning in with a slow, deliberate sniff.

The scent hit him instantly—brimstone, concentrated and acrid.

He recoiled.

Stephanie startled. "What's wrong?"

He answered without thinking. "It's a gate to hell."

"What?" she gasped.

Aaron cursed himself silently. Too much, too fast. But she'd already walked through the damn thing; lying now would only confuse her more.

"If you and your friend went through that door," he said evenly, "then you went to hell. The door's cursed. It creates a path there."

"Oh." A thin, flattened sound. Her expression barely moved.

Shock again—but this time, deeper. Numb.

Aaron hesitated before speaking the next truth. He didn't like saying it, but he didn't believe in cushioning reality, not when it could get someone killed.

"Your friend is probably dead."

He braced for collapse. Panic. Screaming.

But Stephanie only exhaled, slow and hollow.

"I thought so," she whispered. "I couldn't feel her in my heart anymore."

Aaron's stern expression softened. "Are you okay?"

She studied him then—really studied him—as if finally registering the gravity written across his face. Tears welled, but she held steady.

"Yeah," she said. "I just hope she didn't suffer."

"Most people wouldn't handle it that well," Aaron admitted, retrieving something from an inner pocket.

"Why shouldn't I?" she asked quietly. "Freaking out won't change what happened."

"No," Aaron agreed. "It won't."

He moved to the sink, turned the water on, cupped some in his hand, and lifted it to his mouth. When he had enough, he uncorked the vial and let a single drop fall in. Then he faced the door.

He sprayed the diluted holy water across its surface.

A violent hiss erupted—black smoke curling upward like burning tar—and then the cursed residue dissipated.

Stephanie stared. "What was in the vial?"

"Holy water," Aaron said, slipping it back into his jacket. "Diluted, but enough to break the curse. We needed that. Otherwise we weren't walking out of here—this door would've always led back to hell."

Stephanie's confusion hardened into anger. "I lost my friend because someone cursed a door?"

"Pretty much." He pushed the door open. "Come on. We've still got one more of your friends to find."

She followed, still shaken, still trying to reconcile everything she had missed.

Aaron wished he knew the kids' names. It would've made explanations easier.

"The last one I saw was the kid with the glasses and the Letterman jacket," he said.

"Henry," Stephanie answered quietly.

Aaron shook his head. "I guess. I don't know the kid's name."

Stephanie accepted that and let him take the lead. He paused at the men's restroom door, then slipped inside with his revolver drawn. After what happened with the women's room, he had Stephanie hold this door open from the outside. When he emerged, he could already feel the curse radiating off it.

"That one was cursed too," he said as they moved on. "Didn't find your friend in there. Hopefully he didn't go through it."

He found a piece of debris and wedged it under the door. "If it's open, they can't come back through from hell."

Stephanie didn't understand every detail, but she grasped the implication. "Where are my friends now?"

Aaron stopped and looked over his shoulder. "I left them in the garage next door. That's where I'm taking you—and Henry."

They lingered in the hallway, Aaron slightly ahead of her, poised to move the second they stepped back into the open floor. He wasn't risking another kid slipping away. Once he got them all secured—or out entirely—he'd sweep this place clean. Demons first, explanations later.

He didn't like cockroaches. Demons were just cockroaches with better PR.

Henry was the tricky part. Aaron had seen him heading toward the restrooms earlier, but then the chaos with Babs and the two demons pulled his attention. Stephanie hadn't seen anything—she'd been trapped by the cursed door.

If Henry had stumbled through that hell-gate...

Aaron didn't finish the thought. The kid had either survived a miracle or he hadn't survived at all.

He intended to give the boy the same miracle Stephanie had been granted—whether she realized it or not.

He scanned the bar floor, revolver up, Stephanie close behind. Two escape routes: weave through the pool tables toward the front door—slow, risky—or cut back to the bar, then up the center aisle. Indirect, but clear.

"Stay on me," he told her. "And whatever happens, don't stop."

She nodded, and they moved.

At the bar, Aaron shifted her in front of him—she'd be safer ahead while he covered their retreat. He would hold the rear guard until she reached the front doors, then cross behind her.

But before they made it ten steps, everything fell apart.

"Stephanie!" a strained whisper came from the shadows.

She froze.

Aaron cursed silently as Henry crawled out from beneath a pool table, his glasses askew, eyes wide with terror. He had seen Aaron enter but hadn't known the man was looking for him. Seeing Stephanie had drawn him out.

And Karen was not far behind.

Aaron had paused behind the bar, intending to reposition once Stephanie reached the exit. The decision saved her life.

Karen erupted upward from the other side of the bar like a puppet yanked on razor wire. Her face—once lovely—was warped into something masklike and crawling, reshaped by whatever lived beneath her skin. She leveled a shotgun down the aisle.

She hadn't expected Aaron to be on her side of the bar.

"Get down, Stephanie!" Aaron barked.

Stephanie didn't think—she dropped instantly, hitting the sticky floor hard.

The shotgun thundered. Pellets tore through the air where her head had been half a second earlier, shredding the bar's front doors into splinters.

Aaron fired the same moment the blast finished echoing. His round met the shotgun as Karen tried to chamber another shot. The weapon split cleanly down the middle, the metal shrieking apart from the force.

Karen snarled, fury twisting what remained of her human expression. Then she dropped behind the bar in a blur that was too fast, too wrong, too fluid to be human.

Aaron squeezed off another round, but she was gone before the muzzle flash died.

"Move!" Aaron snapped, voice cutting through the chaos.

Stephanie jolted up and sprinted away from the front door on pure instinct—an instinct that saved her life. Three large knives struck the door a heartbeat later, burying themselves deep into the wood. Had she run straight for the exit, at least two would have sunk into her spine.

Aaron fired again. Karen vanished behind the bar with inhuman speed, his shot chewing splinters from the counter instead of demon flesh.

He spat a curse, then another, each one punctuating his rising irritation. He hated missing. Hated slippery targets. Hated demons who refused to stand still and let him shoot them in the forehead. He even briefly considered asking Karen to do just that—but she didn't give him the chance.

She vaulted the bar in a blur, landing in a predatory crouch, machete raised. Aaron offered a silent thanks to whatever powers might be listening: at least she hadn't armed herself with another gun.

Close-quarters. Fine. He could work with that.

Karen struck first, forcing him into a tight defensive rhythm. Her machete slashed, stabbed, carved—blindingly fast. Instead of firing, Aaron had to use the revolver itself as a parrying tool, metal clanging against metal as he redirected her blade again and again.

He felt like deli meat under a rabid butcher's knife.

Twice he tried to fire point-blank. Twice he had to abandon the shot at the last instant to block a lethal stab instead. Professional frustration coiled hot in his chest—he needed one clean second, one clear opening.

The opening arrived from an unexpected direction.

A pool ball whistled past his shoulder.

Karen sliced it out of the air with such casual precision that the deflection almost looked choreographed. But it cost her: for a fraction of a second, her blade angled away from Aaron.

He swung his revolver up—

—and she still managed to bring the machete back into line. It was almost miraculous.

Aaron really hated that.

He fired anyway, but the shot veered wide as he was forced to twist the revolver across his body to block another downward cut. Her blade hit the barrel hard, shoving it sideways and pinning his arm across his chest. The gun was trapped. His right arm useless. His stance compromised.

Karen paused, savoring her advantage. Her eyes glowed a deep, hell-born crimson as a gloating, gravelly laugh escaped her twisted mouth. She thought she had him cornered—pinned and about to be butchered.

She had done exactly what he'd wanted.

Aaron's smile widened by degrees.

Confusion flickered across Karen's features a split second before she felt the cold metal press against her chest.

She looked down—too late.

"Who told you I only had one gun?" Aaron asked.

He pulled the trigger.

The shot lifted her off her feet. Her body twisted midair, wrapped instantly in violent green fire. The stink hit a second later—sulfur, rot, wyrmwood. When the flames collapsed into a puff of black smoke, nothing remained but ash.

Aaron lowered his left-hand revolver and turned toward Henry, who stood frozen near the pool tables, the pool ball he'd thrown nowhere in sight.

"Thanks for the assist, kid," Aaron said, catching his breath. He holstered the revolver on his right hip, then slid the second one into the hidden holster in the center of his back.

"How'd you know I needed the distraction?" he asked as he checked himself over for injuries.

Henry approached, dead serious. "I didn't. I was actually trying to hit her."

Aaron stared at him, then barked out a laugh and clapped him on the shoulder. "Well, thanks anyway."

He moved them toward the exit, scanning the bar for any remnants of danger. Satisfied there were no more surprises lurking, he gave them precise instructions on how to approach the garage without drawing attention.

After Stephanie and Henry slipped inside safely, Aaron covered their rear and followed them in.

The garage interior was dim, but he instantly noted the room's configuration. Babs sat beside a resting—and badly injured—John. Stephanie rushed to her in a tearful, relieved embrace. Henry knelt by John to check on him.

But one face was missing.

Aaron's expression sharpened. "Where's the black kid?"

Babs didn't speak. She didn't need to.

She lifted a trembling hand and pointed toward a bloodstained jacket lying on the concrete floor near the dark mouth of the automotive bays.

Chapter Twelve

"What happened?" Aaron hissed, teeth clenched tight. The anger in his voice wasn't for her—it was for the situation spiraling out of control around them.

In the dim garage light, Babs had trouble seeing the details of his face, but she could read the tension in the set of his jaw and the throbbing at his temples. Her sniffling slowed as she forced herself to breathe, to steady her voice enough to answer.

"He... he went out to the automotive bay to find something we could use. To fight with. To defend ourselves."

She faltered. Her shoulders shook. Aaron stepped closer and pulled her briefly into his arms—unexpected for her, but she melted into the sudden safety. When he released her, she drew a shaky breath and continued.

"He said he'd be right back. Then he left through there."

She pointed toward the shadowed opening leading into the bays.

"He was gone maybe ten minutes. Then I heard something—loud. Like metal falling or something breaking." Her throat worked, remembering. "I called out to him. He didn't answer. So... I finally went to look."

She turned her face away from the bloody jacket on the floor.

"I found that. Just the jacket. I picked it up and brought it back."

Aaron's gaze slid to John. The boy hadn't moved, still propped where Babs and Chris had left him. No new injuries, no worsening condition. Good enough—for now.

He returned his focus to Babs.

"Did you see or hear anything else?"

She shook her head firmly. "No. The door out that way is still barred. Nobody went past me." A beat. "All the windows are boarded up too."

Aaron raised an eyebrow, impressed.

She'd been terrified, but she'd still paid attention. That mattered.

"I'm guessing you didn't search the whole place?" he asked gently.

Babs wrung her hands so hard he worried she'd pop a knuckle. He reached out, touching her fingers lightly. She stilled, then met his eyes.

"No," she whispered. "I was too scared."

Aaron gave her a warm, earnest smile.

"I'm glad you didn't. Going alone would've been suicide. And if something happened to you, there'd be nobody here to look after your friend."

He gestured toward John.

Babs blinked, surprised to be praised for what she thought was cowardice. Stephanie looped an arm briefly around her shoulders in silent support.

Aaron headed toward the dark opening leading into the bays.

"I'll be right back," he promised, locking eyes with Babs so she knew he meant it. "I'm going to find Chris. You all stay here. No wandering. I don't want to lose anyone else."

Stephanie stepped forward before anyone else could respond.

"I'll keep everyone here. You go handle the rest. We'll be right here waiting," she said, voice steady.

Aaron paused, studying her—recognizing the spark of strength, the resilience that reminded him of a woman waiting for him at home.

Then he nodded once and disappeared into the shadows.

Stephanie exhaled slowly, the weight of sudden leadership settling over her shoulders. She hadn't asked for it. She'd never led anyone in her life. But Aaron had trusted her. And the others were looking to her now, whether they said it aloud or not.

She straightened.

First priority: John.

She crouched beside him, assessing the injury as best she could. Babs explained everything she and Chris had done. Stephanie checked his temperature first, relieved to find no fever. She examined the dressing next—clean enough, secure enough, at least for now.

Good thing those health and safety classes she and Babs had taken last summer weren't a complete waste. Tonight, they were all she had.

And maybe... more than enough.

With John as stable as their circumstances allowed, Stephanie settled beside him, propping him against the wall. She took several deep breaths, trying to wrestle the chaos of the night into something she could process. Questions stormed through her mind, all pointing toward the one person who might have answers—Aaron.

Babs eased down beside her. A quiet understanding passed between them, as if both girls needed the presence of someone familiar to stay grounded.

Stephanie noticed Babs was still without her cheer skirt—just her bloomers now—and it nudged her to ask. The conversation came easily then, because what else was left but the truth? Babs recounted everything: John's injury, her own attack, and Aaron's sudden, impossible rescue.

Then she asked the question she'd been avoiding—Quinn.

Stephanie tried to tell it all. Every detail. Every impossible shift in reality. Every second of the terror that still clung to her skin. She spoke clearly but without emotion, as if her mind had gone numb in order to keep functioning.

And inevitably, the conversation came to Chris.

Babs shifted closer, trying to offer comfort she had no idea how to give. She knew how deeply Stephanie cared about Chris—everyone knew. Losing someone you loved... Babs couldn't even imagine it. She glanced at Henry on the other side of John and admitted privately, If something happened to him, I'd fall apart.

She marveled at Stephanie's composure.

"Stephanie... I wanna go home." Babs' voice cracked, the tremble in her words betraying how close she was to breaking.

Stephanie wrapped an arm around her, pulling her tight. "I know," she murmured. "I do too."

Across from them, Henry remained quiet. He had settled beside John, ready to help if the injured boy stirred. He listened to everything the girls said, processing it all, waiting for a moment when his words might matter. But for now, silence felt kinder.

He wanted to go home too.

They all did.

The door opened, and Aaron stepped back into the room. All four kids immediately straightened, hope rising like a breath held too long. But Aaron returned alone. And he didn't wait for them to ask.

"I didn't find anything that could tell me what happened to your friend," he said flatly. "I think he might be dead."

Stephanie absorbed the news with the same steady resolve she had shown earlier. There would be time to fall apart—if they survived the night. For now, survival came first.

But she needed answers. Not out of curiosity—out of necessity. They couldn't navigate this nightmare blind.

She turned to Aaron.

"Who are you?"

"My name is Aaron," he replied, as if the name alone should explain everything.

It wasn't enough. Not even close. She raised an eyebrow at him, but the dim lighting robbed the gesture of impact. So she tried again—directly this time.

"What I meant was: What's happening? How are you involved? And why are you here?"

Aaron's lips curved into a knowing smile.

"I figured that's what you were really asking. I just needed a minute to figure out how to say all this in a way you'd understand. And believe."

Stephanie glanced around. No one else seemed inclined to speak. So she continued.

"At this point, I think we'll believe almost anything. Tonight has been utterly fucked." She paused. "Excuse my French."

Aaron didn't bother to sugarcoat anything. He dove straight in.

"The city of Ionia is cursed," he said.

Babs blinked. "I thought that was just something adults said to make the place seem mysterious."

He shook his head. "No. It's real. And I think you've already seen part of it. 'All roads lead to Ionia'—it's not a slogan. It's a barrier. It keeps people from leaving. And it all started with an angel trying to get back into heaven."

Stephanie stared at him. After everything she'd seen tonight, she still struggled.

"How does an angel cause all this?" she asked. "Aren't angels supposed to be... good? How could one be responsible for what's happening here?"

"Angels are agents of good," Aaron began, "but this particular angel got cast out of heaven. In trying to claw her way back in, she created the curse—and opened a portal to hell. That's what the demons are using to cross over in larger numbers."

His hand rested unconsciously on the butt of his revolver. He wasn't threatening them; rather, some instinctive connection tugged between him and the weapon—an unspoken readiness he couldn't explain even if he tried.

Stephanie absorbed this slowly. "So if an angel opened the portal... what can we do?"

"You? Nothing." Aaron's voice was calm but resolute. "But I can. That's why I'm here. My job is to kill anything that's crossed over and then destroy the portal they used to get in. But this isn't a one-time problem. It's happening all over the city."

Aaron rose from his crouched position and walked toward the boarded window. He peered through the slats, scanning for movement—any silhouette that shouldn't be there.

"We need to get you kids out of here," he said.

Stephanie joined him at the window, anxiety heavy in her voice. "Do you really think we can make it out with those things still roaming around?"

The neon spill from the bar painted them both in a warped glow. Aaron nodded.

"If I can get you to a vehicle, you can escape. Once I destroy the altar, the nearby gateways—the cursed doors like the ones in the restrooms—will collapse. The demons won't be able to cross through."

"But there are still a lot of demons," Stephanie pressed. "Especially those bikers."

"I know. And I'll handle them. It's easier if I'm alone. Hard enough fighting demons without having to protect four untrained kids."

Stephanie took a breath, processing all of it. Then: "Okay... so how do we get out?"

Aaron pointed toward the line of vehicles outside. "I'll give you cover. You get one running, pile in, and drive. Fast."

Stephanie's mind jumped immediately to the bloodstained jacket and Chris's keys. She hesitated—neither she nor Babs could stomach the sight—but Henry could.

"Henry," she called, "can you check Chris's jacket for his keys?"

Henry understood without needing her to explain. The gore didn't faze him—not physically at least—but knowing it might be Chris's blood made his stomach lurch. He crouched by the jacket, searching every pocket.

"No keys," he said after a moment.

He paused, thinking. Then he checked John's pockets—and found them.

"Got 'em." He tossed the keys to Stephanie, who caught them easily despite the low light.

"Alright," Aaron said, "let's move."

Stephanie and Henry helped John to his feet. Sweat slicked his forehead, and every smallest movement sent pain knifing through him. Stephanie wiped his brow with her sleeve, murmuring reassurance even as fear curled in her gut—he needed real medical help, and soon.

Aaron led them outside. Stephanie and Henry flanked John as he staggered across the gravel lot, each step a struggle. Babs followed close behind.

They reached John's truck. Stephanie handed the keys to Babs. "Open the door for us."

Babs hurried ahead, swung the door open, and Stephanie climbed inside first to help pull John up from within. Henry boosted from the outside, and after a few agonizing seconds, they managed to get him into the seat. Babs slid in next. Henry vaulted into the truck bed. Stephanie slipped into the driver's seat and reached for the keys as Babs passed them back.

She turned the key.

Nothing.

No click. No grind. Not even the pathetic wheeze of a dying starter. Just silence.

Her brow furrowed. She checked the gear. Checked the ignition again. Tried a third time.

Still nothing.

Her heart dropped.

Outside the truck, Aaron continued scanning the lot, every sense tuned for the slightest hint of movement. When the engine failed to start a third time, he moved toward the driver's side, expression taut.

Stephanie struggled with the window controls until finally giving up and pushing the door open.

"What's wrong? Why aren't we moving?" Aaron asked.

"I've been trying!" Stephanie snapped, more frustrated than angry. "The damn thing won't start. I think it's dead."

Aaron studied her for a beat. "Pop the hood."

He holstered his revolver as he walked around to the front. Stephanie pulled the release lever, and the hood jolted upward. When Aaron lifted it fully, the sight inside made him mutter a sharp, "Damn."

Stephanie hurried around to join him.

"What—" she began, but Aaron cut her off.

"They got to it before we did. Sabotaged it. They knew we'd try to escape."

Stephanie's voice cracked with frustration. "So what do we do now?"

Aaron opened his mouth to answer—but Stephanie suddenly went rigid, her eyes widening in horror as she looked past him.

"Aaron—behind you!"

He spun instantly, instincts firing. But even with the warning, he wasn't quite fast enough.

The pickaxe came down hard.

It slammed into his right shoulder with a meaty, sickening thud, forcing him to stagger backward. Pain exploded across his chest and arm, but Aaron's training took over. Even half-falling, half-stumbling, he managed to draw his revolver.

His fingers were already going numb, his grip slipping—but he still squeezed the trigger.

The demon shrieked as the bullet struck home, erupting into a column of green fire. The stench rolled across the lot, less concentrated in the open air but unmistakable. The creature collapsed into burning ash as Aaron hit the ground, the revolver tumbling from his fading grip.

"Damn," he breathed through clenched teeth.

Stephanie sprinted to him and crouched beside him. "Are you okay?!"

Aaron didn't answer at first—just reached up with his left hand, yanked the pickaxe from his shoulder with a sharp grunt, and reclaimed his revolver.

"We need to go," he hissed. "Now. That thing screamed. The others heard for sure."

He forced himself upright, swaying for a second as the pain pulsed down his arm. His eyes flicked to the gravel beneath them, a distant, absurd thought crossing his mind—*'Wasn't this lot paved earlier?'*—but the pain crashing through him shoved everything else aside.

He steadied himself.

"Get everyone ready," he ordered. "We're running."

Part Four
Chapter Thirteen

Stephanie crouched beside Aaron, extending a steadying hand as he fought to find his footing. From the passenger side of the truck, Babs emerged—small, shaken, but determined. For a moment she stood frozen, confusion pinning her in place, until instinct finally kicked in and she joined Stephanie without a word.

Aaron's balance faltered again. His legs refused cooperation, buckling beneath him. Babs slipped to his opposite side, bracing her shoulder against his. With his right arm injured beyond usefulness, she wrapped both her arms tightly around his waist, contributing every ounce of strength she had.

Through gritted teeth, Aaron hissed, "We gotta get outta here. Now."

His gaze never stilled—scanning the shadows, watching the open lot, searching for demons that might emerge at any second. He needed to check his arm, the damage, the bleeding—anything—but the kids came first.

Stephanie instinctively began guiding them toward the abandoned garage. Aaron halted her with a small shake of his head. She stopped dragging him forward. He tipped his chin in the opposite direction.

"Head to the motel," he whispered. "It's closer. I booked a room before I went into the bar. We can use that."

It was enough. Stephanie and Babs adjusted course, helping him toward the motel. Stephanie glanced back toward the truck, wanting to call out for Henry but terrified of drawing attention. Her worry eased when she saw Henry climbing down from the truck bed. Their eyes met—he would follow.

Babs hurried ahead as soon as Aaron regained enough control of his legs to manage with only Stephanie's assistance. He pressed the room key into her palm and told her the number. By the time Stephanie and Aaron reached the door, Babs already had it unlocked.

They had barely made it inside when Henry slipped in behind them and shut the door quietly. He moved immediately to the window beside the door, easing the curtain back only enough to peer through. Satisfied with whatever he saw outside, he turned his attention to the room—and immediately noticed someone missing.

"Wait... where's John?" Henry asked.

Everyone exchanged confused looks.

Aaron let out a sharp, exhausted snort. "What is with you kids and always leaving someone behind?"

With urgency, Stephanie said, "Henry, didn't you help John out of the truck when you climbed down from the bed?"

Henry shook his head quickly. "No. I checked the truck before I followed you guys. He wasn't in it. I figured he got out with Babs. Thought he was ahead of you."

Stephanie's eyes snapped to Babs.

Babs's voice trembled. "He didn't get out with me. He was still sitting in the truck when I climbed out. I didn't see him after that."

Stephanie exhaled a quiet, frustrated sigh. She guided Aaron to sit on the bed—he was in no condition to stand, let alone fight—and then turned toward the door with crisp determination.

Aaron's voice stopped her. "Where you going, girl?"

She pivoted, jaw set. "I'm going to get my friend."

Aaron closed his eyes briefly and shook his head. "I'll go get him." He attempted to push himself upright, but his legs betrayed him. He dropped back onto the bed, the effort leaving him breathless.

Stephanie rushed to steady him. "How exactly do you plan to find him like this? You can't even stay on your feet. You're bleeding everywhere. I need to look at your shoulder before you pass out."

She reached for his jacket, fighting his stubborn resistance.

Henry stepped forward. "I'll go find John, Steph."

Stephanie froze. Henry was right—it had to be someone else. "Alright... but not alone."

Before she could volunteer herself, Babs stepped in front of her, a small hand catching Stephanie's wrist. "I'll go with him. You patch up Aaron. We'll be fine, and we'll come back as soon as we find John."

Stephanie's shoulders sagged—not with defeat, but with relief. "Be careful. Take the key. Come back fast."

Babs squeezed her arm once in reassurance and followed Henry out the door.

Stephanie turned back to Aaron, who sat slumped on the edge of the bed, watching her with half-lidded eyes. She seized his jacket again.

Aaron resisted. Again.

Frustration burst through her exhaustion. She threw her hands up.

"Why won't you let me help you? Why are you being a stubborn, obstinate ass?" she snapped, exasperation echoing in every syllable.

Aaron's expression shifted into something close to relief the moment Stephanie dropped her hands and stopped trying to peel his jacket off. Carefully, he pushed himself upright again—but even standing was a struggle. His posture listed noticeably to the right, and he paused midway through straightening, meeting Stephanie's glare.

She stood planted, arms crossed tightly across her chest, lip jutting forward, eyes narrowed. "Are you that determined to stop me from helping you?"

Aaron exhaled, still not fully upright. "Probably about as determined as you are to help me."

"What the hell is that supposed to mean?" she shot back, stepping toward him. "You're bleeding. We need to take care of that now."

Aaron's left hand twitched as if to reach his right shoulder, but the motion died halfway and fell back to his side. "I know. And I can handle it myself."

He angled toward the bathroom—only to stop when Stephanie squarely blocked his path.

Her tone turned mocking. "Really?"

Before he could react, she lifted his right arm a mere inch.

Aaron sucked in a pained, muffled cry.

"How exactly do you plan to take care of it yourself," Stephanie asked sweetly, "when you can't even lift your arm?"

Aaron glared daggers at her. "You're evil, girl."

"Just let me help." She reached for his jacket again—determined, relentless.

Aaron put out his left arm, barring her with a firm but shaky block. "Wait." He drew in a slow breath. "You're about to see something... different when my shirt comes off. Might surprise you."

Stephanie stared at him like he'd just claimed water was wet. "I've seen demons explode into green fire tonight," she said flatly. "I literally walked in hell. At this point, I doubt there's anything left that can shock me."

Aaron studied her—really looked at her—to see if she meant it. When he was satisfied, he lowered his arm and straightened as best he could. Standing at full height, he had an inch or two on her, and she had to tilt her chin up to hold his gaze.

"Just giving you fair warning," he said quietly. "What you're about to see can be... overwhelming."

Stephanie rolled her eyes, a crooked smirk forming. "Let me be the judge of that."

This time Aaron didn't resist as she unbuttoned his shirt and worked his jacket off his arms. It was slow, deliberate work. Every shift of fabric sent a wince across his face, especially on the right side, and Stephanie's movements softened in response. She hated causing him pain, hated that she couldn't stop it—but she kept going gently, steadily.

Most of the bleeding had slowed; by some miracle, the pickaxe had missed anything vital. Finally, Stephanie slid the shirt off his uninjured shoulder—only for Aaron to stop her with a small turn of his head.

"You sure you want to do this?" he asked, his voice low. His back was turned, the nape of his neck the only visible skin.

Stephanie hesitated—not out of fear, but out of curiosity. "Is it some kind of scar you're worried about?"

"No. Nothing like that."

"Alright," she said softly. "I've got this. Don't worry."

He nodded once.

Stephanie pulled the shirt off the rest of the way, freeing his injured arm last, carefully extracting pieces of fabric stuck to dried blood. Then she stepped back to actually look—searching for scars, burns, strange markings. Anything that would justify his dramatic warning.

But there was nothing. Aaron looked—aside from the knife wounds, claw marks, fresh injuries—entirely normal. Or at least, as normal as someone with his build and presence could be. She opened her mouth to ask what all the fuss had been about—

—and Aaron rolled his shoulders.

The sound was wrong. A series of deep, organic cracks echoed across his chest—like bones flexing in ways bones shouldn't. He rolled them forward, ignoring the pain entirely.

Stephanie froze.

Then she understood.

With a ripple beneath his skin, something massive shifted behind him. A shape pressed outward, then unfurled, and Stephanie's breath caught as two wings—sixteen feet across—burst into the open air, stretching widely into the cramped motel room.

They were feathered, but unlike any feathers she'd ever seen: black as obsidian, yet shimmering at the edges with an emerald sheen, as if catching light that wasn't there.

Stephanie's mouth fell open.

She tried to speak. Failed. Tried again.

"Oh... wow."

That was all she could manage.

And Aaron, wings half-spread, blood streaking his shoulder, stood before her—no longer just the stranger who saved their lives, but something otherworldly.

Something that wasn't supposed to exist.

Henry scanned the expanse of the parking lot, washed in a sickly neon glow. Nothing moved. No silhouettes. No shifting shadows. No sign of John.

His gaze drifted toward the truck. From this angle, the interior was a black void—no way to tell if anyone sat inside. Behind him, Babs clutched his hand so tightly her knuckles trembled. Her small fingers dug into his palm with desperate strength, but Henry didn't mind. Her grip steadied him as much as he steadied her.

If Henry was the courage, Babs was the heart—and right now they both needed each other.

He gave her hand a comforting squeeze. "Come on," he whispered.

They moved, half-crouched, half-running, crossing open ground with nothing to shield them but darkness. Out here, they were exposed—if anything watched from the bar or from between the buildings, they would be seen instantly. Henry quickened the pace, pulling Babs with him.

When they reached the truck, Henry pressed Babs behind it and positioned himself as a shield. John had parked facing the bar, casting a deep shadow behind the truck—just enough cover for two terrified teenagers trying to keep each other alive.

They crouched there, breathing fast and shallow.

Henry leaned out first, inching his head past the bumper. The passenger door gaped open, swallowing the cab in darkness.

He ducked back.

"I'm going to check the inside," he whispered. "Stay here and watch for... anything."

Babs gave him a deadpan look. "This whole *thing* is 'anything,' Henry."

He allowed a small, dry smile. "You know what I mean."

She rolled her eyes but nodded. "Just hurry."

Henry inhaled, then broke from cover in a quick sprint toward the open door. He slid to a stop beside it, braced a hand on the frame, and peered inside.

Empty.

A curse almost escaped his throat, but he swallowed it. How the hell had they lost John? It made no sense. He backed away and returned to Babs, kneeling beside her again.

"He's not there," he murmured. "I don't know where else to look. We should go back, tell Stephanie, make a plan."

Babs hesitated—then shook her head.

She peeked around the truck, eyes narrowing toward the abandoned garage. "If John got confused and didn't see us run to the motel... he might've gone back to the only place he knew. The garage."

Henry joined her, thinking it through. "Yeah, but what if we get separated from them? If something happens—"

Babs looked back toward the motel, then back at Henry, her face only inches from his.

"I'd rather not run back and forth across this parking lot twice," she said softly. "We're already here. Let's check the garage once. If he's not there, then we go straight back."

Henry's pulse jumped—not from fear, but from how close she was. She squeezed his hand again, firmer this time.

"You sure this is what you want to do?" he asked. Part of him feared she'd say yes, because that meant leading her deeper into danger.

But her eyes didn't waver. "I'm sure. I want to get this over with and leave this whole place behind."

A small smile tugged at his lips this time.

"Alright. Let's go."

Babs grinned back, determination lighting her expression. She lifted her hand slightly, waiting.

Henry intertwined his fingers with hers, and she held that moment for half a heartbeat—just long enough to anchor herself—before tugging him forward.

They ran.

No shadows moved. No demons appeared. No sounds broke the silence except their light footfalls and their quick, anxious breaths. Reaching the garage felt like a small miracle.

They stopped just outside the open rear entrance, catching their breath. Henry raised a finger for silence and stepped forward first.

He peeked in.

Dark. Quiet. No movement.

"Let your eyes adjust," he whispered.

Babs nodded, stepping close—so close her shoulder brushed his arm. The only way in or out was the entrance they stood in, and the darkness inside felt heavy with possibility. She reached for Henry's hand again, fingers trembling from cold and fear.

He didn't pull away. Instead, he let her wind her arm through his, nestling herself against him as if hiding within his shadow. Her bloomers offered no warmth, and fear did nothing to heat skin—but Henry's presence did. He didn't mind her closeness. He didn't find it awkward. If anything, he tightened his arm just slightly, grounding her.

Together, they waited for their vision to adjust to the dark maw of the garage.

And then—they stepped inside.

Henry's presence wrapped around Babs like a small, private sanctuary—warm, steady, and painfully familiar. She leaned into him the way she always had, wishing the comfort could quiet the ache she'd carried since middle school. Her love for him ran deep, woven into every version of herself she'd grown into.

But as they crept deeper into the garage, searching for John, the question she'd avoided for years clawed its way back.

Why had nothing ever happened between them?

Why, when he knew how she felt, did he never choose her?

Finally, she couldn't keep it in.

"Henry," she whispered, careful not to let her voice echo. "What's the deal with us? You know how I feel about you. Why won't you just be my boyfriend?"

Henry froze mid-step. He didn't answer—not directly. But he'd heard her. The small hitch in his stride told her as much.

When he finally spoke, he dodged.

"Well... John likes you. I don't know what he's planning. He hasn't—"

Babs yanked his arm, hard enough to stop both of them.

"Stop," she snapped. "That's not what I asked. And don't change the subject. Why do you keep acting like something's going on with you and John? He started bullying you after freshman year and you let him. And you keep pushing me toward him. But he's never liked me. I know that for a fact."

Henry avoided her eyes, shoving his glasses up the bridge of his nose—his tell. Stephanie had never told Babs what the tell was, but she'd picked up on it anyway.

"There's nothing going on between me and John," he muttered.

Another lie.

Babs stepped closer, close enough to feel him tense. She lifted his hands and wrapped his arms loosely around her waist. Then she set her hands behind his neck, pulling herself up to her toes.

Her voice trembled with longing.

"Everyone always says I'm the prettiest girl in school, Henry. But I only ever felt beautiful when you looked at me the way you did back in middle school."

She swallowed. "I just... want to be your girl. I've always wanted that."

And before she could think better of it, she kissed him—soft at first, then deeper, desperate, trying to break through whatever wall he kept between them.

Henry didn't push her violently—just firmly, gently, the way someone stops a door from closing on their fingers. He stepped back, breaking the kiss.

Her tears caught the faint light, silver streaks on her cheeks.

"Why?" she whispered. "Why don't you love me anymore? What did I do wrong?"

Henry removed his glasses slowly, folding them with careful precision.

"You didn't do anything wrong, Babs."

"Then tell me what's happening," she insisted. "Why is there this... distance?"

He inhaled shakily, then let out a long breath.

"Babs... I need to tell you something. John isn't picking on me. We've been pretending."

Her confusion was immediate.

"Pretending what?"

Henry rubbed the bridge of his nose.

"John and I have been... together. For about two years."

A thin, wounded sound escaped her—half gasp, half cry.

"You're telling me you and John are dating?" she whispered. "All this time? And you couldn't tell any of us? You couldn't tell me?"

Her hands hit his chest—small, shaking blows that barely hurt but carried everything she felt: betrayal, heartbreak, humiliation. She wasn't angry that Henry loved someone else. She was angry she'd been left in the dark while loving him so openly.

Henry waited, letting her vent, before carefully taking her wrists.

"We didn't want anyone to know," he said softly. "If the guys on the team found out, they'd... make things hard. And we weren't ready for all that."

"That's not the part that hurts!" Babs cried. "You knew how I felt. You let me keep wondering why I wasn't enough. Why you didn't want me."

Henry reached toward her, wanting to pull her into a hug—but she stepped back sharply.

"Don't," she warned. "Please don't."

"Babs... I didn't know how to tell you," he said, voice cracking despite himself. "That's why John and I pulled away from the group. We weren't trying to hurt you."

She shook her head slowly, staring at the floor. Her fists clenched, then loosened as defeat settled over her shoulders.

"You should have told me, Henry," she said quietly. "I deserved that much."

She turned toward the garage entrance.

"Babs, wait—"

"You can find John on your own."

Her voice was cold, steady, and final.

She didn't look back.

And she didn't stop walking.

Chapter Fourteen

Stephanie stood frozen, eyes wide and lips parted, utterly stunned by the enormous wings unfurling behind Aaron. They weren't illusions. They weren't tricks of the dim motel lighting. They were real—massive, feathered, living things that moved with slow, effortless grace. The tips flexed and shimmered like polished obsidian dipped in emerald light.

After everything she'd seen tonight, she still felt foolish for doubting her own senses. Yet here she was, staring at actual wings on a human being.

Her hand rose toward them instinctively. But just inches before contact, fear jolted through her, and she snatched her hand back.

Aaron noticed and folded the wings partially, making himself smaller.

"You can touch them," he said gently. "They won't hurt you."

Stephanie looked from his eyes to the wings again. "Are they... real?" she whispered.

Aaron let out a low, surprised laugh. "As real as anything else in this insane world."

She steadied her breath and extended her hand once more. Her fingertips grazed the nearest feather—warm, smooth, and softer than she expected. A faint tingling shot up her arm, but it wasn't unpleasant.

"How... how is this even possible?" she murmured. "Are you human?"

He blinked, momentarily thrown. "I hope so," he said with dry humor.

Realizing she'd spoken her thoughts aloud, Stephanie flushed and hurried on.

"How did you get wings? Are you an angel? Can you fly?"

"Hold on," Aaron said, raising a hand—though his right arm barely moved thanks to the wound. Stephanie instantly understood and stopped her barrage.

"One at a time."

She nodded, still staring. "Can you fly?"

"Not fly," Aaron admitted. "My bones are too dense, my muscles too heavy. But I can glide."

"Wow." The word escaped without permission. "So... you weren't born with them?"

"No." He exhaled heavily. "The story behind them isn't pretty. I was given these wings for a specific job."

"What job? And who gave them to you?"

"You've already seen it," Aaron said. "I hunt demons. And close portals when they appear."

He lowered himself so she could reach his injured shoulder again. Stephanie resumed her examination carefully, her hands steady despite the storm of questions in her head.

"I didn't ask for wings," he added quietly. "Or this job. But I didn't get a choice."

"So who gave them to you?" Stephanie pressed.

Aaron didn't flinch. "Samael," he murmured.

Stephanie blinked. A flicker of confusion crossed her face.

"Lucifer."

Stephanie froze mid-motion. Her hands hovered over his wound before slowly retreating.

"What?" she breathed.

"Yes," Aaron said simply. "The Son of the Morning Star cursed me."

Stephanie's eyes darted from his wings to his face and back again.

"This is a curse? Why would something evil give you... this?" She gestured helplessly at the wings, still unable to find a word grand enough.

Aaron suppressed a laugh, though it tugged at the corner of his mouth.

"I think you're misunderstanding Samael."

Her brows knit tightly.

"How can anyone misunderstand the devil? He's evil. God cast him out of heaven. Isn't that the whole thing?"

Aaron shook his head slowly.

"He was cast out, yes. But the idea that this makes him automatically evil is... oversimplified."

"How?" Stephanie demanded.

"Samael didn't rebel because he wanted to overthrow God or become evil," Aaron said. "He rebelled because he refused to accept that angels should kneel to humans—creatures made of flesh, born to die. That defiance got him banished. And afterward, God put him in charge of hell. Someone had to keep demons contained, punish the wicked, keep the order of things down there."

Stephanie stared at him, trying to connect the version of Samael, or rather Lucifer, she'd grown up with to the one Aaron described.

"And this has what to do with you?"

Aaron's gaze drifted toward the wall for a moment, as if remembering something he wished he could forget.

"Even though Samael governs hell," Aaron continued, "that doesn't mean he controls every demon. They obey him when it suits them. He can destroy the disobedient, sure, but he's not omnipotent."

He grimaced, voice dipping closer to a mutter. "And he's an insufferable asshole who doesn't know how to take 'no' for an answer."

Stephanie blinked. "That is... the strangest thing I've ever heard."

She tied off the bandage on his shoulder, scrutinizing the injury. "This isn't as bad as I thought."

"It was," Aaron said, glancing away. "It's already healing a little. Give it a few days."

He watched her closely, waiting for the moment she registered the implication.

"That's incredible," Stephanie muttered, dry skepticism sliding in. "Convenient perk when your job is demon-hunting."

Aaron chose to ignore the sarcasm. "Useful, yes. But I still can't use this arm." He attempted to flex his right hand; the fingers barely twitched. "Everything's numb."

Stephanie stepped around him as he shrugged back into his shirt, still waiting for him to clarify. "So what does that mean? Because you're definitely telling me that for a reason."

Aaron gave a crooked smile. With an awkward, left-handed reach, he drew his revolver from the holster on his right hip. "You're quick."

He held it out to her.

Stephanie handled the weapon without hesitation.

"My dad was military," she said. "I grew up around firearms. Safety first, always."

She lifted the revolver, checking the iron sights with practiced ease. "He also taught me to shoot," she added. "I was good."

Aaron nodded once. "Good," he echoed.

By the time he finished slipping into his jacket, the wings were gone—as if they'd never existed.

"Let's go get your friends," he said, moving toward the door. Stephanie followed, revolver in hand.

As soon as they stepped into the walkway, they spotted Babs approaching from the lot. Her steps were small. Her expression was wrecked. Tears had carved thin, shining paths down her face.

Babs brushed past Aaron without a word and walked straight into Stephanie's arms.

Stephanie hugged her immediately, instinctively, one arm wrapped around Babs while the other kept the revolver angled safely downward. Over the top of Babs' bowed head, she exchanged a look with Aaron—silent, uncertain.

"Hey, girl," Stephanie murmured, her voice soft. "What's wrong? And where's Henry?"

Still pressed against her chest, Babs mumbled, "I told that big jerk to find John on his own."

Stephanie stroked her hair once, then looked to Aaron again. He looked just as confused.

"Okay... then why the tears?" Stephanie asked gently.

"I don't want to talk about it," Babs said, her voice cracking.

So Stephanie didn't press. She held her for a few long, steady breaths until Babs finally nodded against her.

"Feel better?" Stephanie asked softly.

"...Yeah," Babs sniffed. "Thanks for being here."

When Babs stepped back, Stephanie shifted to business. "We need to find Henry and John. Now."

Babs wiped her face and gave a weak, but determined, smile. "I'm ready. Let's go."

Aaron spoke up. "Let's find the one whose location you know first. Where'd you leave Henry?"

"In the garage," Babs said, pointing toward the dark silhouette of the structure. "He's probably still in there looking for John."

Aaron nodded and immediately took point. Stephanie and Babs fell in behind him, sticking close as they crossed the parking lot. Stephanie kept the revolver angled low but ready, every sense alert.

Aaron's head was up, scanning every shadow. "More demons have crossed over by now," he murmured to himself. "I need to find that portal and shut it down. Then I can clean up whatever's left."

When they reached the back of the garage, Aaron lifted his hand, signaling them to freeze. They obeyed instantly.

He listened.

Voices.

Faint, muffled—but moving closer.

Someone inside the garage was headed toward the rear exit.

Stephanie strained to parse the muffled voices inside the garage. She couldn't make out the words, but she recognized Henry's cadence—the clipped consonants, the nervous uptick at the end of sentences. He was getting closer to the door.

So when Aaron motioned for her and Babs to silently retreat back toward the parking lot, her mind scrambled to understand why.

Henry was clearly coming. And if Henry was talking to someone, that someone had to be John.

But Aaron signaled again—sharp, decisive, fingers slicing the air.

Stephanie didn't argue. She didn't understand, but she obeyed.

Something primal inside her trusted Aaron without being able to articulate why.

Only when Henry emerged did Stephanie understand.

He stepped into view with John beside him...

Except it wasn't John.

The shape, the height, the voice—the imitation was flawless. But everything about it made Stephanie's nerves crawl.

Her brain couldn't pinpoint the detail that gave it away, but her instincts screamed the truth: 'That thing wasn't John.'

Aaron felt it too.

Babs, unfortunately, did not.

"Henry! John!" she called out brightly, waving as if nothing were amiss. "I see you found him after I left!"

Henry jumped, clutching his chest. "Jesus, Babs—you scared the shit out of me."

Stephanie threw out an arm, stopping Babs from rushing forward.

Confusion flashed across Babs' face, but Stephanie couldn't explain—not before Aaron stepped in to handle it.

Henry's eyes darted between the three of them—the guns, the tension, the way both Stephanie and Aaron stood like they expected an attack.

"What's going on?" he asked, unease bleeding into his voice.

Aaron raised his left arm, aiming the revolver at Henry—not at him but past him. "Henry. Come here. Right now."

Henry froze. "Why? What happened? Am I missing something?"

Stephanie lifted the revolver Aaron had given her. Her tone was low, precise, each word a hammer-blow:

"That. Is. Not. John."

Henry spun around instinctively—

—and that was the end of him.

The thing behind him seized both sides of his head and twisted.

The wet, violent crack echoed across the lot.

Babs shrieked, the sound raw and animal. Stephanie yanked her close, clamping a hand over Babs' ear, turning her away from the sight.

She couldn't protect Babs from the sound, or the smell—but she could shield her from seeing what was left of Henry.

The demon—still wearing John's face—tilted its head. "What gave me away?"

"Your stench," Aaron spat.

The demon grinned.

Another shape lunged out of the garage darkness.

Aaron didn't hesitate—he fired, the revolver bucking hard in his left hand. The second demon went up in green fire, its scream slicing the air.

"What the hell?" Babs cried, shaking violently in Stephanie's arms.

"I don't know," Aaron replied, "but we've got company. We need to move. Now."

Stephanie held Babs tight as she backed them away. "Where are we going?"

Aaron didn't waste breath answering. He pointed across the lot, and they ran.

A shotgun blast exploded behind them just as they reached John's truck. Buckshot peppered the metal with pinging impacts; one tire hissed as it went flat.

Aaron rose, fired two shots, ducked back down.

A demon screamed.

"There's about a dozen by the building," he reported.

Stephanie popped up beside him, fired two lightning-fast rounds, and dropped two more demons in green flame.

"Looks like ten now," she said with a grim little smile.

Aaron stared at her—was that admiration? Jealousy? Both?

He settled on grateful.

Behind the truck, Babs trembled violently. Stephanie hugged her once and whispered, "You're safe. I've got you," then forced herself back into combat mode.

From across the lot, the John-demon called out sing-song:

"Hey, Stephanie... are you going to answer me?"

Aaron shook his head sharply. "Don't. He's stalling."

Stephanie knew he was right.

She answered anyway.

"What the fuck do you want, you filthy piece of shit?"

Aaron blinked at her—less shocked by the decision to respond than by the language.

The demon continued, voice dripping with poison.

"I just wanted to say I'm sorry about Henry. I wanted to make him last. Like John. You should've heard John beg—"

Stephanie didn't let him finish.

She sprang up and emptied four shots in rapid succession, firing so fast that fire guttered and demons screamed before the demon could finish his taunt.

Flames lit the lot like sickly green lightning, then snuffed out.

"I'm out of bullets," Stephanie said, snapping the cylinder open and finding it empty. "Got any more?"

Aaron gave a short, humorless laugh. "Nope."

Chapter Fifteen

Stephanie fixed a perplexed gaze on Aaron, her brows furrowing as though he'd just spun an absurd tale. Surely she'd misheard him. Or maybe he had misunderstood her. How could anyone walk into a fight with demons without carrying extra ammunition?

It made no sense. She couldn't assume he knew in advance exactly how many rounds he'd need. Stephanie had zero experience in demon hunting, but even she understood how ridiculous it would be to run into danger underprepared. To her, it bordered on idiocy—and that frustration burst out of her in a single, unfiltered demand.

"What the fuck do you mean you don't have any more goddamn rounds? Are you fucking stupid?"

Aaron blinked at her, wearing a strange mixture of confusion and mild amusement. "There never were any bullets in these guns to begin with."

Stephanie stared at him, her mouth opening and closing in dumbfounded silence. A full minute passed before she finally found her voice again.

"Then how—how in the world have we been using them to kill demons?"

Aaron only shrugged, clearly reluctant to waste time answering this particular question. They didn't have the luxury of pausing for a detailed lecture, and they both knew it.

"With faith," he said simply. "You just have to believe."

Stephanie looked down at the revolver in her hands, the weight of it suddenly strange. Skepticism flickered across her features, but something else followed—an acceptance she couldn't fully explain. She turned the gun over, absorbing the truth she hadn't asked for and wasn't sure she wanted.

"Now you tell me," she muttered.

"I didn't say anything earlier," Aaron replied, "because if you didn't believe, it wouldn't have worked for you." He lifted a hand toward the weapon. "Now you understand that all you need is... faith and trust."

The glare she leveled at him could have stripped paint. "That wasn't fair."

Aaron's grin showed zero remorse. "But it worked. Now—shall we deal with these demons?"

Stephanie gave Babs a steadying nod, patting her shoulder in a silent command to stay put. Then she met Aaron's eyes again. He lifted his hand, counting silently.

Three. Two. One.

They rose together and unleashed a coordinated storm of fire.

Within seconds, only a handful of demons remained. The last six fell quickly—two to Stephanie's precise shots, the rest to Aaron's. When the echoes faded, they stepped out from behind the truck, surveying the burned, stinking aftermath.

Babs crept out from her hiding place. "Was that... was that all of them?"

Aaron slid his revolver into the hidden holster at the small of his back. "That handled the immediate threats."

Stephanie blinked at him. "What's with the cryptic answer?"

Aaron nodded toward the garage doorway. "Remember the portals?"

"Yeah," she said, tension in her shoulders. "You mentioned that already. So—is that why you're being vague now?"

"In a way," Aaron said. He glanced at Babs and gently pulled her against his side to steady her. "Until we find the main portal and destroy it, more demons will keep crossing through. Pain, misery, and grief—all on repeat."

Stephanie shifted her focus between them. "So where do we start looking?"

Aaron pointed toward the garage. "A portal needs an actual doorframe. I checked this whole building already. That leaves the bar and the motel."

Stephanie stiffened. "Wait—the men's room you said was a gateway to hell... is that the portal?"

Aaron shook his head. "Those were secondary gateways. The main portal will have an altar next to it—the place where the spell was cast. To shut down every secondary gate, we have to destroy the main one. The portal, the altar, and the demon who opened it. If that demon lives, it can just open another portal somewhere else."

Babs peered up at him. "So... how do we find the demon?"

"If it doesn't want to be found," Aaron answered, "we won't. We can only hope it hasn't finished whatever mission it came here for."

Stephanie exhaled sharply. "So they actually have a plan? A mission?"

Aaron downplayed it with a shake of his head. "Not a complicated one. They're collecting souls to take back to hell and consume."

Stephanie's voice trembled with a mix of anguish and outrage. "Does that include my friends—the ones those bastards killed?" The thought turned her stomach. Fury simmered under her skin. The idea of her friends being food for demons was almost too much to bear.

Aaron, unflinching, delivered the truth. "That's usually what happens. Samael doesn't allow unnecessary suffering—so demons can only feed on the misery of souls they bring to hell. If Samael doesn't know a soul is there, he can't protect it."

Stephanie growled in frustration, stomping her foot with enough force to echo across the lot. Aaron noted—again—that the parking lot had returned to asphalt. Reality continued to shift in small, inexplicable ways.

Her outrage poured out. "Don't they already have enough souls from the wicked? Isn't Samael supposed to torment the damned?"

Aaron shook his head. "He punishes evildoers only to the degree of the evil they committed. Souls thick with darkness don't offer much sustenance. Demons crave the ones with more light. But Samael sends the souls with too much light for hell—but too much darkness for heaven—to purgatory. Souls with even more light never go anywhere near hell. So demons corrupt a soul, drag it across, and hunt."

"This is insane." Stephanie raked a hand through her hair. "So now we're... food? This sucks!"

Before the spiraling frustration could swallow her, Babs cut in, her voice soft but steady. "So... where do we start looking for this altar and the main portal?"

Aaron shifted his gaze toward the bar. "I checked the restrooms earlier—nothing there. But I didn't get a chance to search the kitchen or the office. It's smaller than the motel. Easier to rule out."

He looked between Stephanie and Babs, waiting for objections. None came. In truth, he'd been planning to keep them behind—safe, armed, out of harm's way. But Stephanie beat him to the punch.

"How about you check the bar," she offered. "I'll take Babs back to the motel room and wait for you."

The offer slid neatly into the space where his plan had been forming, and yet—something felt off. Too convenient. Too fast. She had understood his intention before he voiced it, and that raised a flag he couldn't ignore.

He narrowed his eyes. *'Does she plan to search the motel alone?'*

She had the skill to keep herself and Babs safe. That wasn't the concern. The problem was that only he knew how to destroy the portal. Only he knew what the altar would look like. Only he could finish the job.

As if she sensed his suspicion, Stephanie spoke up quickly.

"If you're worried I'm going to take off by myself, stop. I'll wait for you. Promise. But I need to get Babs somewhere warm." She cast a glance at the shivering girl. "It's freezing out here."

Relief washed through Aaron. Stephanie wasn't scheming—she was protecting. Prioritizing Babs. That mattered more than anything.

Aaron looked down at Babs and noticed she was still holding onto him—not out of fear, but because she was cold, dressed only in the remnants of her cheer uniform from the encounter with Tank and Romeo.

Her face brightened at Stephanie's suggestion. Aaron nodded. "I'll meet you in the room. Clear it first. Don't let Babs inside until you know it's safe."

With their plan set, the three split off—only temporarily—until Aaron finished his sweep of the bar.

He watched the girls retreat, then turned toward the entrance. His right arm throbbed dully, improving but far from full strength. His hand remained numb. He smirked to himself, thinking of the word sinister—Latin for "left," later twisted to mean "malevolent."

'Left-handed work indeed,' he thought.

As he approached the bar door, a thought whispered through him: *'We need not assume a sinister motive for these endeavors.'* The irony wasn't lost on him.

He pushed the front door open with his right arm, revolver ready in his left. The interior was unchanged from when he'd last emerged with Henry and Stephanie—except the stench was gone. The thick stink of brimstone and wyrmwood had dissipated after the earlier fight. Three neat piles of ash lingered near the front—human-shaped shadows of the demons, Tank, Romeo, and Karen.

To his right, the pool tables stood silent. The corridor leading to the restrooms sat empty; the men's room door remained propped open, indicating nothing was coming through its secondary gateway.

On the left side of the bar stood the double swinging doors to the kitchen—the only way to reach the back of the building.

Aaron swept the room with a practiced eye. The kitchen seemed an unlikely place for an altar or a main portal, but he refused to dismiss any possibility. On top of the double doors, only two other potential rooms existed: a back door, and a small office.

He checked the office first. Nothing. Empty.

Then he approached the back door. He didn't need to open it. He could feel it—sense it. If the door connected to hell, he wouldn't need to turn the handle.

It didn't.

Initially, Aaron's heart sank. The altar's presence—something he had sensed the moment he entered the bar—still pulsed faintly in the air, yet the altar itself remained nowhere to be seen. He swept the kitchen again, eyes narrowing. Then his gaze settled on the walk-in freezer.

'Of course.'

If someone wanted to hide an altar in plain sight, they would choose a place few would willingly inspect—cold, isolated, sealed by a door within a frame. A perfect disguised portal.

Determination surged through him as he gripped the handle and swung the freezer door open.

A wall of stench slammed into him so violently he nearly gagged. The air was thick with the sickly-sweet rot of decomposing flesh. Even without looking, he could feel it—the altar's malignant aura radiating from within.

He stepped into the freezing chill.

The altar sat directly in front of him, and upon it lay a grotesque arrangement: a heap of human intestines, haphazardly coiled, with a severed head nestled atop them like a macabre centerpiece. Aaron's stomach twisted—entrails and head belonged to the same person, no question.

The head was turned away from him. Fighting the wave of rot-induced nausea, he moved closer and gently angled it toward him.

The damage of decay hadn't yet erased the features—this altar couldn't have been here for more than a week.

Recognition struck like a blade.

Aaron swore—loudly, vividly, creatively—because he knew exactly whose face stared back at him.

No time to linger. He dug into his jacket, pulled out a small vial of holy water, and doused the altar in a swift, practiced motion.

The reaction was instant.

The spell ruptured with a violent hiss, sending a plume of dark smoke billowing upward as the altar's connection to hell severed. Aaron spun toward the exit—

—and froze.

The kitchen was on fire.

Not a flicker. Not a small blaze.

A full inferno.

Flames roared across the walls and ceiling, racing toward him in a hungry, coordinated sweep. Heat slammed into him like a physical force. Smoke curled thickly, choking the air and blotting out the room beyond the doorway.

A trap.

Set on the altar.

Rigged to ignite the moment someone destroyed it.

His right arm throbbed. His lungs burned. Vision blurred from the smoke. No path forward. No path back.

He scanned desperately—and then spotted salvation: an access panel overhead leading to the roof.

Without hesitation, he climbed onto the nearest counter, coughed through a lungful of smoke, and shoved the panel up with all the strength he had left. Cold night air hit him like a blessing.

He pulled himself through the opening.

But safety was an illusion.

He emerged onto the roof of a derelict building, flames devouring the interior beneath his feet, the structure shuddering with each new pulse of heat below.

The bar was burning from the inside out.

And Stephanie and Babs were waiting for him in a motel that might already be under siege.

Stephanie and Babs returned to the motel room without encountering any more demons—a stroke of luck that gave Stephanie a flicker of confidence. Maybe they'd be safe long enough for Aaron to finish at the bar and come back for them.

Once inside, Stephanie ushered Babs through the door and excused herself to use the bathroom. She set the revolver on the bed and peeled off her jacket, tossing it carelessly over the firearm and burying it from sight. As she headed toward the bathroom, her body cracked and popped with each stretch.

"Man, I'm beat. I wish I knew what time it is," she muttered, closing the bathroom door.

Babs, acting on instinct, pulled her cellphone from her pocket to check the time for her exhausted friend. Her fingers froze.

The phone wasn't dead.

She frowned, head tilting as a fleeting memory brushed the edge of her awareness—something about the phone. Before the thought could crystallize, a noise erupted behind her.

"You—" Babs gasped.

A hand struck her across the head, sending her crashing between the twin beds. She hit the floor hard and didn't move.

A moment later, Stephanie emerged from the bathroom, too focused on drying her hands with a towel to register anything out of place. She assumed Babs was right where she'd left her.

"Did you say something, Babs? I couldn't hear you over the fan," Stephanie called out, lifting her gaze—

—and froze.

"Chris?" she breathed, joy bursting through her chest at the sight of the person she loved standing there, seemingly unharmed. She took one eager step forward...

...then stopped.

That feeling.

That same awful prickle of dread she'd felt when "John" appeared behind Henry.

"You're not Chris," she said flatly.

A slow, impossible grin crawled across the demon's borrowed face—too wide, too wrong for human anatomy.

"You're right," he purred. "I'm not Chris." He gestured lazily toward Babs' unconscious body on the floor. "Your friend figured it out. Your stranger friend almost did too, but I slipped away before he could."

Stephanie's gaze darted to Babs, relief washing over her at the sight of her chest rising and falling. She wanted—desperately—to check on her. But moving toward Babs meant moving closer to the thing wearing Chris's face.

That wasn't happening.

"What did you do to Chris?" she demanded, the worry breaking through her voice.

The demon chuckled, a low, mocking rumble.

"Now you care about Chris? Now you care about anyone besides yourself?"

"What are you implying, demon? I've always cared about my friends," Stephanie snapped. The towel slipped from her fingers as her fists clenched, knuckles whitening.

With no escape route behind her, Stephanie had no choice but to stand her ground. Her muscles coiled tight, jaw locking as she prepared to fight if she had to.

The demon saw the change in her posture and smiled wider.

"Is that so?" he taunted. "Henry couldn't reconcile his feelings for her—" he pointed at Babs "—or for John. John struggled with his own identity. Babs worried no one would ever see her for who she is instead of what she looks like. And Quinn? She just wanted to be more than the trophy her parents paraded around."

Each truth hit Stephanie like a blow. The words were too sharp, too precise—things she'd sensed but never fully understood. Her fists loosened, fingers trembling.

The demon noticed immediately.

And he pressed the advantage.

"Did you ever truly know these things about your friends?" the demon pressed, twisting the emotional blade deeper.

Stephanie fought the instinct to bow her head and break. All night she had locked every shard of grief behind a wall just to keep moving. Survival had left no room for mourning. Now this creature was trying to tear that wall apart—force her to drown in emotions she wasn't ready to face.

But surrendering meant dying.

And she wasn't ready to die.

"I know that if my friends ever needed me, all they had to do was ask. I would've been there for them," Stephanie said, forcing steel into her voice. She refused to let him rewrite her truth.

"Really?" the demon murmured, taking a slow step forward.

Stephanie instinctively backed away, heel brushing the edge of the bed—right where her jacket hid the revolver.

"What about Chris?" the demon continued. "Did you ever understand how badly he needed you while he was fighting with his father? He cried himself to sleep, praying you'd ease the pain. Eventually he stopped asking for help—because he realized you were never coming."

His voice slithered across the room, thick and oily.

A storm surged inside Stephanie—fury, grief, guilt, all crashing violently against the fragile walls she'd tried to hold up. Seeing Chris's face twisted into this monster's expression only made it worse. Chris, the person she would have died for. Chris, who had always pushed everyone away—and she had let him.

'I should have been there anyway.'

Her own inner demons chimed in, cruel and familiar.

'I should have tried harder.'

"Chris loved you deeply," the demon added, driving the knife home.

Stephanie snapped her head up, eyes blazing. "I did my best. And I won't let you make me responsible for his death. I assume you're the one who killed him."

The demon wrapped his arms around himself and laughed—a sound like bricks grinding together.

"Oh, indeed I killed him," he said with gleeful malice. "And I savored every moment."

Stephanie's fists balled, tears streaming freely now. She wanted nothing more than to smash the smug smile off his stolen face. She braced herself to try—

But the door exploded inward.

Aaron barreled into the room.

The demon's head whipped toward him, giving Stephanie a sliver of an opening. She lunged for the jacket, fingers closing around the hidden revolver.

The demon spun back toward her, torn between threats—and chose wrong.

Stephanie raised the gun Aaron had given her, faith surging so fiercely through her that it felt like fire in her veins.

"I'm sorry, Chris," she whispered, voice breaking. "I loved you so much."

She fired.

For a heartbeat, nothing happened. Higher demons didn't ignite instantly. But it was enough—just enough—for Aaron to grab the collapsing body and hurl it out the door. The corpse hit the concrete just as green fire erupted, devouring it in a rancid inferno.

Aaron was back inside an instant later.

Stephanie shattered.

Her knees buckled, sobs wracking her entire body as she clung to the gun. Gently, Aaron pried the weapon from her hand and pulled her into his arms. She crumpled against him, her grief pouring out in helpless, body-shaking waves.

He held her through it—until the storm eased into quivering whimpers.

Only then did he whisper, soft and steady, "Fold your wings away, Stephanie. Babs doesn't need to see them when she wakes."

Stephanie shifted, glancing over her shoulder at the wings unfurled behind her—her wings, revealed in the chaos without her noticing.

explicitus est liber

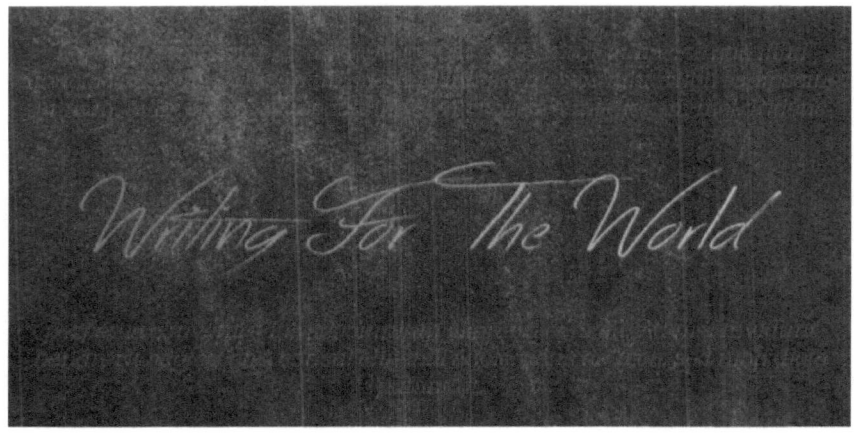

https://writingfortheworldpress.com

Also by J. A. Springs

Chronicles of Cosmic Realms
Shadows of the Forgotten Void

elctrcsheepdrmwrks (Electric Sheep Dreamworks)
Blurred Vision
Fractured
Zero One

Essays in Systems and Being
Essays in Systems and Being

The Absurdities Anthology
How Not to Find Your Local Weed-Man

The Gifted
The Untamed Force
Next Exit

The Shepherd Series
The Bad Shepherd
The Good Wolf

Standalone
Sundrops
Behind the Red Door
Boundless Fragments: A Collection of Novellas and Short Stories
Fragments of Forever

Watch for more at https://authorjasprings.com.

About the Author

I'm J. A. Springs.

Father of six wonderful children. I served twenty years on active duty, living around the world and experiencing things I never imagined I would. I spent time in societies and countries I once couldn't have envisioned as part of my future. I've done a lot—and still not enough.

These days, I live quietly, accompanied by my cats, music, and an interest in writing that consumes me. I've been writing seriously since 2021. I never set out to write in a particular genre—it made more sense to write around them instead. As for goals? There aren't many. Enjoy the first cup of coffee in the morning and see what the day brings.

Read more at https://authorjasprings.com.

About the Publisher

LLC. Lancaster, PA

www.writingfortheworldpress.com

Read more at https://www.writingfortheworldpress.com.